Lord, help me. I'm in love with her.

It was the first time he'd ever allowed himself the full thought, though the emotion had been hovering in his heart for years.

He focused on the distant, shining body of water and beyond to the narrow line he knew to be Redemption River.

"We should head back down."

One hand holding the puppy steady, Kitty said, "You must be starving."

"I could use a bite." *And more space between the two of us.*

"Me, too." She stepped away from the window but lingered in the oddly shaped room for a few more minutes while he stood like a helpless teenager watching and yearning.

"I love this room, Jace. I've never seen anything like it. If I lived in here, I would turn this space into something I could use every day. It's far too wonderful to be hidden away in an attic."

Her innocent phrasing caught in his brain and spun in repeating circles.

If she lived in this house—an impossible thought he'd never get out of his head now that he'd seen her here.

Books by Linda Goodnight

Love Inspired

In the Spirit of...Christmas
A Very Special Delivery
*A Season for Grace
*A Touch of Grace
*The Heart of Grace
Missionary Daddy
A Time to Heal
Home to Crossroads Ranch
The Baby Bond
**Finding Her Way Home
**The Wedding Garden
The Lawman's Christmas Wish
**A Place to Belong

*The Brothers' Bond
**Redemption River

LINDA GOODNIGHT

Winner of a RITA® Award for excellence in inspirational fiction, Linda Goodnight has also won a Booksellers' Best, an ACFW Book of the Year and a Reviewers' Choice Award from *RT Book Reviews*. Linda has appeared on the Christian bestseller list and her romance novels have been translated into more than a dozen languages. Active in orphan ministry, this former nurse and teacher enjoys writing fiction that carries a message of hope and light in a sometimes dark world. She and her husband, Gene, live in Oklahoma. Readers can write to her at linda@lindagoodnight.com, or c/o Steeple Hill Books, 233 Broadway, Suite 1001, New York, NY 10279.

A Place to Belong
Linda Goodnight

Steeple
Hill®

Published by Steeple Hill Books™

STEEPLE HILL BOOKS

Steeple
Hill®

Recycling programs
for this product may
not exist in your area.

ISBN-13: 978-0-373-81533-3

A PLACE TO BELONG

Copyright © 2011 by Linda Goodnight

www.SteepleHill.com

Printed in U.S.A.

But the vessel he was making did not turn out as he had hoped, so the potter crushed it into a lump of clay again and started over.

—*Jeremiah* 18:4

For His glory. Always.

Chapter One

The day should have been perfect, one of those freshly-washed days after a spring rain when buds burst free from winter, birds sing and the world smells green.

Window rolled down and the engine of his Ford Super Duty rumbling pleasantly, Jace Carter was feeling good. Progress on the 1902 Victorian remodel was going well.

Overhanging oaks dappled sunlight onto the highway as he rounded the curve headed toward home. Ahead, a historic bridge spanned Redemption River and led into the small town of Redemption, Oklahoma.

He slowed to enjoy the view of the river, the way the willows wept over the railing, and the bridge itself, hand built by the town's early pioneers. A man who made his living in wood appreciated good workmanship, especially when it had lasted more than a century.

The familiar *thump* of the road projected him onto

the long historic bridge. He was craning his neck toward the rain-flushed river when the unexpected happened. A pair of screaming, water-soaked men bolted over the railing, arms waving frantically.

Jace's heart bolted, too. He slammed on his brakes, yanked the wheel.

"Help! Help us!" Two hysterical men rushed to his window. Pale as plaster, terror dripped from both like the muddy red of the river dripped from their jeans and T-shirts.

Fear prickled Jace's scalp as he listened to a disjointed, breathless rendering of the basics. Their boat had capsized. There was a man in the water. They couldn't reach him.

He slammed the truck into park, killed the motor and leaped out to run down the slippery slope to the river. At first, he saw nothing but the thick, muddy water, swift and dangerous with the swell of spring rains.

"Call 9-1-1." He tossed his cell toward one man and ran with the violent current, searching and praying for a chance to reel in the hapless victim.

His boots slipped. The thick bog slowed his progress. He spotted a red ball cap snagged on a branch. Hope leaped.

With his boot toes clinging to the muddy bank, he stretched. Missed. The swirling maelstrom ripped the cap away.

Behind him one of the men choked, "Jerry. Jerry."

The noise of the current sucked the sound downstream with the red cap. With a sinking heart, Jace was convinced the same had happened to a stranger named Jerry.

By the time emergency vehicles arrived, Jace's legs and lungs ached and he was wet and muddy to the waist. The two survivors wandered aimlessly along the banks in shock and grief of a day that had begun as fun and ended in tragedy.

Within the hour half of Redemption had joined the search. Jace didn't hold out much hope at this point, but there was always a miracle.

"He could be halfway to the Gulf by now."

Jace lowered a pair of binoculars to look into the grim face of Sloan Hawkins. They stood together with other volunteers on the bridge. The preacher was here. So were Trace and Cheyenne Bowman. Cheyenne, a former policewoman, had helped organize the search with efficient skill. The old Dumpster Divers, GI Jack and Popbottle Jones had arrived with the sirens. They knew the river well and were guiding police boaters toward hidden inlets and snaggy coves.

Below the bridge, ATVs revved and spit mud beneath their tires in a desperate attempt to find the man. That was the way of Redemption. People here cared. That warm acceptance was what had drawn him to the little town fourteen years ago when he was searching for a place to begin life for the second time.

Regardless of fatigue and the shivers of cold running from his muddy, wet feet to his torso, Jace couldn't bring himself to leave.

Once, long ago, he'd been drowning, though not in water, and someone had reached out a saving hand. How could he not do the same?

The vision of a red ball cap floated relentlessly in front of his mind's eye. If he'd been a few seconds faster could he have saved a man's life?

A helicopter *chop-chopped* over the water.

A television news van rolled to a stop on the bridge, blocking the slow crawl of traffic to film the beehive of activity. A brunette in a blue News 12 windbreaker stuck a microphone in Jace's face.

"Sir, anything you can tell us about the missing man? Did you see anything? What do you know about the incident?"

Jace shook his head and turned away, lifting his binoculars to scan the scene below. Tension tightened the muscles in his neck.

Sloan Hawkins, a securities expert with experience in handling situations with aplomb, stepped in to answer.

"From all reports, three men were riding the current. They capsized. Two made it out. One didn't."

"Did you witness the incident? Or talk to any of the victims yourself?"

Jace held his breath, hopeful that Hawkins wouldn't point him as out as a possible witness.

"Sorry. Didn't see a thing."

Jace released the breath. Talking wasn't his favorite

activity, especially to strangers. Words could trip a man up if he wasn't careful.

"Do you know the victim? Where are the other two men?" The reporter's quick eyes scanned the bridge.

Sloan deferred, pointing the woman and her cameraman toward the gaggle of police units stationed on the flats directly south of the bridge.

The reporter sprinted away.

"Be dark soon." Jace squinted into the western sky. He dreaded the moment when light would fail and hope would diminish.

By midnight, weary, disheartened searchers began to slowly leave and the search was called off until daylight.

"There's a man down there somewhere." Jace drew in a long breath and repeated softly, "Somewhere."

Sloan clapped Jace on the shoulder. "Come to the house with me. Eat. I know you haven't."

"I couldn't." But he wanted to. He didn't relish being alone on a night when he'd become too aware— again—of his own mortality.

"Sure you could." Hawkins whipped out a cell phone—one of the fancy kind—and touched a single icon. "Annie, I'm heading home. Jace Carter's with me. They're calling off the search for the night." He listened then laughed softly, though his expression was humorless. "Starved. Love you, too."

The endearment made Jace uncomfortable. Or

maybe envious. He'd never had that kind of casual, confident relationship with anyone. Never would.

But he'd accepted his lot in life. He'd created it, and he'd learned to be grateful for what he had. He made one final glance toward the river. Not everyone got a second chance.

Kitty Wainright stirred the pot of chili on Annie Hawkins's beautiful vintage cookstove. "This will taste good to them after being out on that river."

She and Annie, along with Cheyenne Bowman, had been in the middle of planning a fundraiser for the Redemption Women's Shelter when word of the accident had come. Both Cheyenne and Sloan had left immediately to join the rescuers. Annie and Kitty stayed behind with the children, Cheyenne's step-daughter Zoey and Annie's pair, Justin and Delaney. Annie had long ago put the two nine-year-old girls to bed after a call to Cheyenne. The preteen Justin still dragged his feet, miffed at being considered too young to join the search and rescue effort. Annie was allowing the late night as a salve to his wounded pride.

Outside a motorcycle engine rumbled. Justin leaped from the couch. "There's Dad."

He was out the door in an instant.

Kitty smiled inwardly. The snarly boy had blossomed under the tender-tough care of his father.

"I'll set the sandwiches out." As she moved past

the coffee pot to the refrigerator, she hitched her chin. "Do you think they'll want coffee this late?"

"Sloan won't. I don't know about Jace."

"Me, either." A building contractor who'd gone out of his way to help her after her husband's death, Jace Carter had been in Kitty's motel many times, but she couldn't claim to understand him. "He's so quiet."

"Still waters run deep." Annie grimaced. "Sorry. Poor choice of words. Jace *is* cute though. Nice guy, too."

Kitty made a noise of agreement but didn't pursue the conversation. Annie wasn't finished.

"He looks good. Works hard. Obviously thinks you're someone special."

The comment surprised her. "What makes you say that?"

"Oh, come on, Kitty." Annie waved a jar of mayo. "He spends more time at your place than anywhere."

"I run a motel. An *old* motel that needs constant repair."

"Uh-huh. There are a lot of old buildings in this town."

Annie was right. Over a hundred buildings in Redemption were on the National Register of Historic Places and only an expert with Jace's eye and skill could work on them. Kitty's motel, a throwback to the fifties, was not on that list.

"Jace is the original Mr. Nice Guy," she said.

"True. But have you ever considered that he might be the least bit interested in you?"

Kitty's heart bumped. "No."

Annie rolled her eyes. "Oh, girl. What am I going to do with you? You're what? Thirty?"

"Thirty-one."

"There you go." She slapped a plate of sandwiches on the table. "Open those gorgeous baby blues and take a close look at Jace Carter. He's a doll and he has a thing for you."

"Annie, stop. You know I'm not in the market. Never will be." The very idea gave her a stomachache.

Annie quieted. A nurse with a heart as big and warm as the sun, she knew Kitty's history. "Dave was a great guy, Kitty. We all liked him, but he's gone. Has been for a long time."

Kitty bit her bottom lip. Seven years was a long time but memories never died the way Dave had. "I'm not interested in finding anyone else."

"Really?" Annie's compassionate green eyes bore into her. "Think about that, Kitty. Love is a beautiful thing. Too beautiful to live without."

Didn't she know it? Hadn't she had the best in Dave Wainright? Insides squeezing, she tried to laugh off the conversation. "Oh, you newlyweds. All you think about is love."

Annie arched one blond eyebrow but didn't say anymore because at that moment the men trooped into the country kitchen. Fatigue pulled at their faces.

Kitty's stomach quivered oddly when she looked at Jace Carter. She wished Annie hadn't said such a silly thing. She'd never allowed herself to consider

Jace as…well, as a man, but now she couldn't help noticing. Average height, he bested her by several inches. The word *neat* always came to mind when she thought of him. But tonight his usual tucked in, tidied up appearance was disheveled and dirty. His brown hair was rumpled and tagged with dirt as though he'd run a muddy hand through it.

He had the softest, quietest eyes. Hazel she thought, though she'd never noticed before. And he had strong, carpenter hands, a little rough and work-scarred, but capable. She *had* noticed them before, the way he held a piece of lumber almost tenderly as though he could envision the beauty hidden inside. He was an artist with wood.

"You guys okay?" she asked to stop the flow of her thoughts. Annie and her suggestions.

"Rough night." Sloan did the talking.

Sloan Hawkins, dark and dangerous-looking with blue eyes that could melt a rock, crossed the room to kiss Annie's cheek. "Smells good." He smiled a tired smile. "So does the food."

Annie blushed prettily and swatted at her husband. The newlyweds' sweetness put a catch in Kitty's chest. She and Dave had loved like that. She glanced at Jace, saw him avert his gaze. He removed his ball cap, crushing it in those capable, tattered hands.

"I should go. I'm too dirty to be here." The voice was as quiet as his eyes, warm, too, and manly.

"Don't be silly," Annie said. "Kitty, get him a towel, will you, while I put this food on the table?"

"Got it." She hurried out of the kitchen, glad for the momentary reprieve from her own crazy thoughts. She was tired. That's all.

Jace settled into the chair Sloan shoved at him, glad to be off his feet. He was cold to the core. Should have gone home, but when Sloan said Kitty was here, he'd been too tired to resist. Just looking at her helped soothe the ache of these last few hours.

Tonight her hair was swept up in a knot atop her head and held by a black doodad, but he'd seen it down before, long and pale. She was like a fairy tale, a blonde Rapunzel with a hint of Tinkerbell in her heart-shaped face and blue-bonnet eyes. Jace laughed at his fantastical thoughts but thought them again when he saw her coming toward him with a big blue towel.

"I warmed this in the dryer." She draped the heated terry cloth around his shoulders. "You look cold."

He was cold, inside and out. Tonight's failed rescue chilled his soul.

"Thanks. Feels good." The towel smelled good, too, clean, fragrant and warm. Or was that Kitty?

"You really should get out of that wet shirt. Sloan could probably loan you one of his."

The rain had started, a soft drizzle right before they'd given up the search.

"I'm okay." She couldn't know that he would never remove his shirt in front of anyone. Ever. He was modest, yes, but more than that, he was ashamed.

Kitty hovered, and he searched for something, anything to say, but his useless tongue stuck to his mouth. He'd had no one to fuss over him since he was small, and having her bring him a towel or a glass of tea or a cheery smile felt good. Too good to ruin with words.

Ah, who he was kidding? If not for her motel and the work he did there, Kitty Wainright wouldn't give him the time of day. The motel office was a shrine to her hero husband and according to the local gossip he'd picked up over breakfast at the Sugar Shack each morning, Kitty had openly declared herself a widow forever. As was her way, Kitty was kind-hearted and good to everyone. Even a stray dog like him.

Which made them friends and neighbors and nothing else. Ever. He had long ago declared himself a lifetime bachelor, though his reasons were far less heroic than hers. He rubbed at his shoulder and remembered a time too ugly to forget.

"Let's eat." Annie waved her hand over the steaming bowls of chili she'd set at each place. "There's plenty. Hope it doesn't keep you up all night."

They chuckled at the joke, knowing it wasn't indigestion from the spicy chili that would keep them awake tonight.

They ate in silence until Justin broached the topic of tonight's tragedy. "Do you think they'll find him?"

Sloan laid aside his sandwich, chewing thoughtfully. "Drowning victims are usually found."

"But not always?"

"No. Not always."

Annie shuddered. "Gruesome."

"I wonder if he has a wife and family," Kitty mused and Jace turned to look at her. "I remember when Dave was killed. The army sent an officer. Who tells a civilian's wife?"

"The police."

Annie said, "I wonder if it's on the news."

"Should be. There were reporters everywhere." Sloan trekked over to the counter where a small TV hung from the cabinet. He positioned the screen toward the table.

In the months since Sloan Hawkins, purportedly the bad boy of Redemption, had returned to his hometown and married his high school sweetheart, Jace had come to like and respect the man. There was darkness in him, a darkness Jace recognized because of his own shadows, but Annie Markham Hawkins and a relationship with God had smoothed some of Sloan's rough edges.

Jace knew about that, too—the lightening of dark places with faith. He'd be a dead man without Jesus.

A half-dozen fast-paced, loud commercials flickered across the screen while Sloan surfed through the channels in search of late-night news.

"Here we go," he said, tossing the remote to the table as he returned to his food. "Chili's good, Annie girl. Just what I needed." He winked and squeezed her hand on the tabletop.

Jace suffered the familiar pinch of envy. No man was an island, or some such proverb.

"Hey, Dad. There you are!" Justin leaped up from the table to point. Sure enough, the camera scanned the scene at the river, then focused on Sloan's face. Relieved that he didn't appear in the shot, Jace listened as a digital Sloan repeated his comments to the reporter. He'd no more than thought the thought when there he was. The shot was only a flash as the camera panned but enough for him to recognize himself. Not once, but twice as the cameraman surveyed the rescue attempt.

"You look handsome, handsome," Annie said, smiling at Sloan.

Sloan thumped a fist against his chest. "Hollywood will be calling. What do you think, Jace? Me and you. Made for TV?"

Jace forced a laugh as the rest of them chuckled at Sloan's attempt to lighten the situation.

But chili curdled in the pit of his stomach. TV was the last place he wanted to be.

Chapter Two

Four days later Redemption still buzzed with the tragedy. The rescue had been scaled back, renamed a recovery effort, and moved downstream.

"Horrible," thought Kitty as she whipped sheets from the bed in Unit 7 and tossed them in with a pile of towels for the laundry. The unit had been occupied by a reporter who'd decided the story was over and rushed off to film tornado devastation up in Cleveland County.

Linens in arms, Kitty left the scrubbing for later and stepped out into the spring sunshine. The morning was golden, though the weatherman said more rain was coming. Her fingers practically itched to be digging in the planter boxes and tiny gardens around each unit, but the ground was too wet. She sniffed the scents of grass and damp earth.

Up on the highway a trucker geared down with a low whine, a sure sign he was entering Redemption, not leaving. Maybe he'd stop in for a room. She could use the income.

From the roof of Unit 2, the *whoosh-bang* of a nail gun told her Jace Carter was on the job.

Kitty turned toward the sound, dropping the linens in the laundry room on her journey.

Balanced on his knees atop the roof of Unit 2, the quiet carpenter placed a nail gun against a shingle and fired. Her motel was old and the roof of this room hadn't withstood the test of last week's downpours. The inside was a mess, too.

"Good morning." She shaded her eyes against a stunning glare and looked up.

She could barely see him. Just the curve of his back and the rubber-gripped bottoms of his work boots.

With a skitter and crunch of feet and knees against old-fashioned asphalt shingles, Jace came into view. Moving with studied care and smooth athleticism toward the edge of the roof and the extension ladder, he lifted a gloved hand.

Backlit in sunshine, tool belt low on one hip, brown hair neatly spiked and gleaming clean, Jace wore old jeans and a white and gray striped shirt. She'd never seen him in anything but neatly pressed long sleeved shirts. He was, she realized, a good-looking man.

Kitty ground her back teeth, annoyed at herself and at Annie for putting the notion into her head.

"Morning," he said, voice low and soft. "I hope the noise didn't wake you."

"No. Of course not. I'm an early riser." She figured

he knew that already as much as he'd worked here. When he made a reach for the ladder, she stopped him. "Oh, don't let me bother you. I only wanted to say hi and ask if you'd like coffee or something."

"Got my thermos, thanks." He smiled, a slow, almost cautious response that crinkled the weathered edges of gentle hazel eyes.

"How's it coming?"

Jace was an excellent builder, a restorer of antique homes and furniture. He had far better jobs than repairing her cranky old lady of a motel. Yet he never turned her down. She'd never wondered about that before, but after Annie's comments, she did.

"The roof's pretty old."

Kitty gnawed a bottom lip. "You saying I need a new one?"

"I can make it work."

She knew he could. Jace was a wonder with the historic buildings in Redemption. Though Redemption Motel was certainly not a turn-of-the-century Victorian bed-and-breakfast. It was an old relic of the fifties, cranky, bothersome and a ton of never ending work. And she loved it. More because of who it represented than what.

"I've been thinking of renovating."

Jace shifted. The tool belt dangling on one hip clinked, metal against metal. "Yeah?"

"Thinking." She laughed. "No money for serious renovations."

Motel rooms in a town the size of Redemption

didn't bring in big money. If not for the long-term renters who put regular cash in the coffers, she couldn't keep the doors open. Those and the huge Christmas celebrations, Victorian style, and the Land Run reenactment in April kept the motel afloat. She made enough to get by, but there was seldom any money in the bank for extras. Some extra cash would be a blessing.

"We could work something out. Take care of the major issues. Let's talk about it."

"Okay. I wouldn't want anyone but you tearing into my baby."

Jace was scrupulously honest, always did more than she paid him for, and his work was perfection. Her cranky old lady of a motel looked much better since he'd begun doing the upkeep.

"I'd be disappointed if you did." He hoisted a nail gun toward the graveled lot behind her. "You have company."

Kitty spun toward the sound of tires crunching on the gravel, a sound she acquainted with paying customers. "Come to the office when you finish. I'll fix you a sandwich and pick your brain."

"Can't guarantee you'll find anything."

With a laugh and a wave, Kitty hurried toward the office and the slender man exiting a shiny navy blue sedan.

Jace squinted against the morning sun and watched a moment longer as Kitty's energetic stride ate up the ground. She was easily the most beautiful woman he'd ever known, inside and out. Delicate, feminine, but strong as a willow, she took his breath. Stole his brain cells.

A car door slammed and he heard Kitty's lyrical voice speak to the newcomer though he couldn't make out the words. A man of average height, on the skinny side and dressed in a business suit fell into step beside the cheery blonde proprietress of Redemption Motel. When they reached the office the man opened the old-fashioned screen door and waited while Kitty stepped inside. He followed and the door snicked quietly closed behind him.

A cloud passed overhead, blocking out the sunlight that was Kitty Wainright and setting the parking lot and the motel units in shadow. Jace frowned, gut tightening in the weirdest way. He squinted toward the closed door.

Something bugged him. A fierce, nagging protectiveness welled in his chest. Miserable, hot.

He waited ten seconds. The cloud moved on and he huffed derisively. He'd lived so long on the dark side he was suspicious of everything and everyone.

He bounced the nail gun against his thigh before turning back to the damaged roof.

The suspicions were in his soul, not inside the office of Kitty's motel.

"Ahoy, Jace Carter."

Jace glanced down at the ragged figure of GI Jack and lifted a hand in greeting. The old man dressed in ill-fitting castoffs and an army cap that had seen better days was one of Redemption's eccentricities. Many took him and his partner, Popbottle Jones, for bums. Considering their propensity for Dumpster diving, maybe they were, but Jace found them to be the most interesting bums he'd ever encountered.

GI Jack was an artist, a junk artist who could turn pop cans and wire or cast-off buckets and hubcaps into something beautiful. Jace got that. In a way, finding the worth in the worthless was what he did, too.

Next to the grizzled old man stood a candidate for world's homeliest dog. Most everyone in town knew about GI Jack's pets—mostly strays he'd gathered together over the years. This one was Biscuit, a dog of unknown origins. The only thing Jace knew for certain was that Biscuit was a brown canine with lop-sided ears, oversize feet, and as shaggy as his owner. He looked as if his ears had been sewn on out of leftover parts by a blind seamstress. One flopped low on the side of his head and the other stuck straight up on top. But the dog's tail swished the air with such joyous abandon anyone with a heart would forget his looks and be charmed.

Jace thought of the new puppy at home, a bundle of wiggling joy himself. He didn't know why he'd let the local vet, Trace Bowman, talk him into taking in an abandoned pup. Jace was gone all day, but the pup was sweet company in the evenings. When Milo was older, Jace planned to take him along for the ride.

"Funny that drowning victim has never been found," GI said without preamble.

Jace sighed and shot the nail gun again. The drowned man wasn't his favorite topic. Besides the nagging feeling that he'd not done enough, he'd taken plenty of good-natured ribbing about his cameo shots on the TV news. "Big river."

"That's what Popbottle said. Lots of snags and undertows to drag a man down." GI withdrew a half sandwich from his shirt pocket and took a bite. "The widow's got a leak?"

"More than one."

"You'll fix her up. She's mighty fortunate to have a good builder willing to rush over anytime she needs help."

"Least I can do."

"I figure you got bigger fish to fry than that old roof. Ida June does this kind of repair."

Though past eighty, Ida June Click still worked around town as a handywoman. She was a dandy, too, in her pink coveralls and lime green tennis shoes. "Ida June's getting a little frail to be climbing on roofs."

"Ha! Don't tell her that. She'll challenge you to a roofing contest."

"And win."

"Yep. And win. She's a whirlwind, our Miss Ida June. Reckon you could say the same for our Widow Wainright. Mighty pretty, too."

Jace grunted. Hadn't he been thinking the same

thing? All she had to do was step into view to make his eyes happy. Not that he'd ever tell her that.

"Mmm-hmm." GI's gray head bobbed up and down. "Too bad she's set on being a widow forever. Too young, if you ask me, to give up on life."

"I doubt she's given up."

"Then I reckon you did?" GI cackled at the look Jace shot him. "All right, all right. A shame though, two handsome people, both single and of the same faith—"

Jace pulled the trigger on the nail gun to drown out the rest. After the torment of the last few days— the drowning, the TV picture and noticing Kitty too much—he wasn't in the mood for reminders of his single status. If he ever was.

"Saw that car pull in. Oklahoma plates but not local." GI tore off a bite of his sandwich and handed it to the dog. With delicate nips, Biscuit accepted the treat. "Wonder what he's doing at the motel?"

Jace wondered the same. "Reporter maybe."

"Doubt it."

So did Jace. The drowning story was over for the most part and the news media had departed. "Could be doing a story on the upcoming Land Run celebration."

In late April of every year, Redemption returned to her 1889 roots by throwing a two-day festival that brought tourists and vendors from all over the country.

"Maybe. Looks kind of slick to me. Like a salesman."

"There you go then. Maybe he sells hotel products." Jace shot another nail. "You know, shampoo and soap."

GI scratched the dog's lowest lopsided ear. "I saw some damage on Unit 8."

Jace squinted south toward the mentioned unit. Kitty's motel was old but she kept it up. Rather, he did. Kitty worked around the place, too. She planted pretty flowers and kept everything sparkling clean. There was a long-term renter in Unit 8, and the regulars were the motel's mainstay.

"Yeah?"

"Shingles are off."

"I'm nearly finished here. I'll check it."

"Got nothing else to do, huh? Lazy bum."

Jace chuckled. GI knew better. He was swamped. Always was. He had three other jobs waiting, two in progress, and four more calls to bid before the week was out. He also had his own historic house to finish, an ongoing project for the last three years. He could see the end in sight, though, and was eager to see his dream home come to fruition.

All of them would have to wait though until the motel was taken care of. He felt a compulsion to help anytime Kitty called. He'd begun working on the motel to honor her dead hero husband. Lately he wondered if he'd do the work just for the privilege of seeing Kitty.

"You looking for a job?"

GI barked a laugh. "Jace Carter is a funny man. Well, me and Biscuit got some stops to make. You come on out to the house anytime. I got a new project going. Petunia and Popbottle will be happy to see you."

"Petunia misses me?" Petunia was the resident watch-goat. Last time he'd stopped by to visit she'd eaten his ball cap. The time before she'd nibbled some paint off his truck.

"The old girl loves you, Jace Carter. Bring her a snack anytime."

Jace raised a hand as the eccentric old man shuffled away, lopsided dog at his heel.

He worked for another thirty minutes before checking the damage on Unit 8. Sure enough, a half-dozen shingles were missing. With a sigh, he headed toward Kitty's office to let her know.

He didn't particularly like entering the motel office, but he'd been there plenty of times. He stepped inside, heard the bell overhead jingle merrily, and looked around at the memorial to a man a hundred times better than he was.

Decorated in patriotic colors of red, white, and blue and smelling of flowers, the room was jammed with Americana and military memorabilia. A display case boasted bobblehead soldiers and eagle-topped pens. The walls were plastered with photos, including Uncle Sam who never tired of wanting someone. The pointing finger made him feel guilty.

If he'd been a man, he would have joined the army and fought for his country instead of wasting his youth in trouble.

A tri-folded American flag rested on an enclosed shelf on the wall behind the display. Given the photo of the serious-faced soldier next to it, Jace had long ago surmised the flag had been the one given to Kitty at Dave Wainright's military funeral.

He nodded to the photo, offering his respect and waited for Kitty to hear the bell and come out.

Behind the inner office was the tidy cottage Kitty called home. He'd been inside plenty of times, mostly to discuss repairs of one kind or another, and he'd attended her Bible study on occasion. He'd stopped going to that out of guilt. He had trouble keeping his mind on the Lord with Kitty present and with the memories of her dead husband all around.

He waited, hat in hand, in the outer office. He'd learned patience the hard way, and waiting no longer bothered him.

"Jace, come on back." She rounded the doorframe leading into the back with her usual sunny cheer. All smiles and smelling of roses like the rest of the place, Kitty motioned to him. "Did you finish the roof? I have a check for you on my desk."

He stepped around the display case, avoiding Uncle Sam's stare. "I didn't come for that."

"No?" She paused next to Dave Wainright's flag. "There's damage on Unit 8."

She made a small sound of dismay and bunched her

shoulders. She was so cute when she did that. "Can you fix it?"

"Sure." He smiled, wanting to reassure her. "No worries."

Her smile returned, lighting him up inside. "Worry's a sin."

Right. And he was a sinner.

Kitty laughed, a merry sound like wind chimes. "I have trouble with that one."

"Me, too," he admitted, feeling ridiculously pleased to share such a thing with her. Fact of the matter was, he worried all the time. Though over the years he'd begun to feel safe, a man in his shoes knew not to get too comfortable or too close.

"I'm glad you came in. There's a man in my office who wants to see you."

"Someone needing a remodel?" It happened all the time. He'd be working on one project and someone would stop in and ask him to look at another.

Before she could answer, they stepped into the inner office. The skinny man he'd seen from a distance rose from a chair and turned toward him with a toothy smile.

"Well, there you are. The famous Jace Carter."

All the blood drained from Jace's head. His ears roared and he thought he might pass out, something he'd never done. Not even when he'd been bleeding to death on a cold concrete floor.

He couldn't believe his eyes. He blinked, prayed he was wrong.

He wasn't.

Fourteen years of clean living fell away as he stared into the face of Donny Babcock. A face he'd tried to forget. From a past that had finally caught up with him.

Chapter Three

Somehow Jace managed to shake Donny's outstretched hand. The skin was soft, a clear indication that Donny wasn't doing any manual labor. Donny had always been good at other things besides real work.

"Remember me, old buddy? Donny Babcock?" The toothy grin shone at Kitty in explanation. "Me and Jace go way back. He's surprised to see me after all this time."

A real understatement.

Jace struggled for composure, careful not to reveal too much or to alert Kitty to his discomfort. He stood like a robot, unaffected on the exterior, writhing inside. Dread, deeper than the Redemption well, seeped into his cells.

"A real surprise," he managed.

Donny slapped Jace's shoulder and laughed. The slap was a reminder of what lay beneath his shirt and of the past he shared with Donny Babcock.

"Saw you on TV, Jace old pal. You're famous. A real hero from the sound of it."

Jace regretted every minute on that bridge with TV cameras rolling around him. He wanted to ask straight out what Babcock was doing in Redemption, but he couldn't. Not with Kitty in the room.

"Just doing what neighbors do," he said. "For what little good it did."

"I heard they never found the body." Donny pulled a long face. "Poor man." He glanced at Kitty. "Such a tragedy."

The words were insincere enough that Jace cringed. Kitty didn't seem to notice. She nodded, one hand against her heart in empathy. "I know."

"What brings you to Redemption, Donny?"

"You, Jace old buddy. Well, that and business. I'm in real estate investments now and this area has some interesting possibilities."

"Someone in town told him you might be here," Kitty injected. "Can I get the two of you a soda? Or some tea?"

"Sweet tea from a sweet lady sounds mighty refreshing." Donny dazzled Kitty with another smile. He must have had veneers attached since Jace had last seen him. The smile was too white and big to be natural.

"Nothing for me," Jace said. "I've got to go."

"What's the rush, pal? We need to catch up." Donny slapped Jace's shoulder again. "For old times' sake."

Jace clenched his teeth. If Babcock whacked him again, there would be trouble.

"Of course you do. You two sit down and talk. I'll get some tea." Kitty bustled from the room, leaving Jace alone with his nightmare.

"What are you really doing here?" he growled softly.

"Now, Jacey boy, mi amigo. Is that any way to greet an old friend?" Babcock held up two fingers. "Scouts' honor. My intentions are on the up-and-up. I saw you on TV and figured I'd come down and say hello."

"You've said hello. Now say goodbye."

"Jace, Jace, Jace. You're starting to hurt my feelings. We were good buddies back then. Remember? You and me against the world. Not that I'm one to collect on old debts, but I saved your hide a time or two."

Dark shame flushed through Jace's system. The place on his side began to ache the way it did when he remembered.

"I appreciate it, Donny, I do. But I'm not that stupid kid anymore. I'm a new man, with a good life." Fourteen years of being the best man he knew how to be, of seeking God with all his heart. Of paying penance with every breath in his body.

"And you don't want anyone messing it up. I'm cool with that. I didn't come here to cause trouble for you, Jacey boy."

"Why did you come?"

The toothy smile came again. "To do you a favor."

The sound of soft footsteps stopped the conversation. Jace paced to the door and opened it for Kitty. She carried a tray with two glasses of tea and a plate of cookies. His heart pinched at the kindness. This was the life he'd chosen, the life he'd worked for. Donny was right. He didn't want anyone destroying the respect and friendships he'd gained in Redemption. And Donny's presence threatened everything.

Was he selfish to want him gone? After Donny had been there when he needed him most?

"Let me take that," he said.

Kitty's mouth curved. "Thank you, Jace."

She relinquished the tea and stepped into the room, bringing her fresh rose scent along.

"You shouldn't have bothered. I need to go." He fought to keep his tone easy. "I have an appointment with Samuel Case to bid a job."

He normally wouldn't have explained himself, but today he needed an excuse to get out of here and think.

"But you have a guest."

"No problem, Miss Wainright. Jace and I can reminisce at his place. We were just discussing my accommodations and he insisted I stay at his house for a few days." Babcock turned glittery brown eyes on Jace. "Right, Jace?"

The blatant lie took him aback, but he wasn't ready to call Donny's bluff. Not in front of Kitty. The man knew too much. And he was bound to have a deeper motive for showing up after all this time. Jace had an obligation to himself and to his adopted town to find out what it was.

"You can follow me out to the house."

"No, no, go ahead and bid your job. Old Donny will sit here and enjoy his tea with Miss Wainright. I'll be along later."

"You don't know where I live."

Donny winked. "I'll find you."

Jace's gut tightened. Until he knew what Donny was up to, if anything, he didn't like leaving him alone with Kitty. But he'd backed himself into a corner and could do little else.

On legs shaky with adrenaline, he headed to his truck and prayed all the way to Samuel Case's antique shop.

He should be working, had plenty to do, but Jace couldn't relax until he found out what Donny Babcock was doing in Redemption, Oklahoma. By the time he arrived home from his appointment with Samuel Case, he was drenched in sweat. Worry sweat.

He let himself in through the side door and was met by a delighted puppy. Milo, a beagle mix of some sort with curly ears and soft brown eyes, thought Jace was the sun and the moon.

"Got any presents for me to clean up?"

They were working on house training, and he should probably crate the pup during his absences but he couldn't. The floors were hardwood. They'd clean. No living creature should be locked in a cage.

The dog wiggled harder, mouth open, eyes dancing along with his feet and tail. If a dog could throw out his back, Milo would manage.

Jace crouched on his toes and gathered the bundle of warmth and love against his chest. A few minutes with Milo and he could almost forget his worries.

But not quite. He had a lot to lose with Donny Babcock in town.

With Milo dogging his heels, he paced the gleaming wood floor of his living room. He'd spent hours perfecting this shine. Hours stripping away the old carpet and the old finishes. Layer after layer until he'd uncovered the stunning solid oak flooring, made even more beautiful by age. Someone had told him he should put down area rugs but he couldn't bring himself to cover something this beautiful.

Wood was his passion and nothing fired him up like a piece perfected by age just waiting for the hand of a master craftsman. He frequented estate sales and old barns in search of pieces like the banister now curving toward the second story of the Queen Anne he called home.

He ran a hand over the silky banister. Gary Henderson had taught him to appreciate fine wood, and he'd taught him the skills needed to build a business and a life. He'd also taught him about Jesus. The day Jace had been assigned to Gary's woodshop class had been a blessing he would never take for granted.

It was God, pure and simple, trying to help a messed-up kid.

"You should have known Gary," he told Milo who'd jogged up the stairs to be on eye level with his master.

Jace had taken Gary's shop class to get out of real work. Or so he'd thought. Eighteen years old, he'd been so scared back then any safe place was welcome. And Gary's woodshop was safe. The master builder saw to that. No one monkeyed around under Gary's watch.

"I would be dead without Gary."

He believed the sentiment with his whole heart. With Gary's guidance he'd become a real man instead of a punk kid destined for the cemetery. Gary had been the one who'd urged him to leave the city and start fresh in a place where no one would judge him by anything except his workmanship and character. He'd done that. He'd made Gary proud.

He blew out a worried breath.

More than anything today, he needed to talk to his mentor and friend.

He rubbed a hand over the back of his neck and paced some more. Milo hippity-hopped down the stairs and followed.

Gary was gone. Died two years after Jace moved to Redemption to start over.

"God, you see my dilemma. Guide me." Jace wasn't a big talker to anyone else, but God already knew all his faults and mistakes anyway. And the dog thought every word was meant for him. Milo plopped down on his bottom, one leg sticking straight out as he cocked his head to listen. "Why has Donny Babcock tracked me down? After all this time, it can't be good. It can't be."

He headed into the kitchen, oblivious for once to the granite counters and the warm patina of the hand-lathed cabinets. He should eat something but his stomach gnawed with anxiety.

He thought of Kitty and the gnawing got worse. He shouldn't have left her alone with Babcock. Even if Donny had saved him from a knife-happy convict and certain slaughter, he'd been shady, always working a deal. A con in a building full of cons. Jace didn't want Kitty hurt by anyone, least of all by someone connected to him.

As he reached into his back pocket for the cell phone, a car door slammed. He replaced the phone and went to the door. Donny was already there. He entered the house without being asked, brushing past Jace to gaze around at the inside of the Queen Anne.

"This your place?"

"It is." His and the bank's.

Donny stopped in the foyer, a soaring entry with a stained glass transom and crown molding. "Why didn't you buy something new? Who wants old stuff like this anymore? It's not even finished."

Jace's jaw tightened. "I like it."

Milo, unused to being ignored, yipped once. Donny

stopped dead still, mouth curled in distaste. "You got a mutt?"

Mildly, Jace said, "Meet Milo."

"I don't want dog hair on my suits." He pinched the pleat on his pants, then flecked imaginary hair from his jacket.

Since the last time Jace had seen him, Donny's taste in clothes had gotten noticeably more expensive, though the suit hung on his thin frame like it would on a hanger. His brown hair was slicked back and gleamed with gel, his black patent wing-tips spit-shined as if he'd learned in the military. Which he hadn't. He reeked of department store cologne. All in all, he appeared respectable but Jace worried that beneath the polish beat the heart of the same sleazy hustler who'd conned his own family out of thousands.

Though tempted to tell Donny to find another place to stay, Jace kept quiet. The only motel in Redemption belonged to Kitty.

Ignoring the growling dog, Donny wandered into the next room. The future office was as empty as the living room.

"You need some furniture, pal. What's the matter? Out of cash?"

Jace tried to see the rooms from someone else's point of view. Other than a chair here and there, an antique desk with telephone and computer, and an incredible mahogany sideboard he'd rebuilt, they were basically empty. Even his bed was an air mattress tossed on the floor.

As with everything in the house, Jace wanted authentic pieces. Finding them, refurbishing them took time. He was a patient man who enjoyed the search.

"I can help you with that," Donny pressed. "With the cash flow problem."

"Just tell me what you want, Donny. I know you didn't show up here after fourteen years out of sentiment."

"Tsk-tsk. So suspicious. I told you, Jacey boy, I've come to do you a favor. Let's order pizza and talk over a couple of beers. The widow's tea didn't do it for me."

"No beer." Jace crossed his arms over his chest and leaned against the fireplace bricks. Milo sat on his foot, eyeing Donny with the same suspicion his master felt.

Donny stopped his hyperactive perusal of Jace's house. Shoving back his suit jacket, he propped both fists on his hips. "No beer?"

Jace shook his head. "I'm a Christian now."

"Hey!" Donny lifted both hands. "Me, too."

Jace's heart jumped. He leaned forward, hoping. "For real?"

"Me and the big dude upstairs, we're tight. Yes sir." Babcock held up a pair of crossed fingers. "Just like this. Serious, pal. I got a Bible and everything."

Jace wanted to believe him but the words reeked

of insincerity. That had been the way of the man Jace remembered. A consummate liar, he said what people wanted to hear until he got what he wanted. Then he'd laugh like a hyena behind their backs and call them fools.

Jace didn't want to join the crowd of fools.

"So how about a few beers between a couple of former old sinners?" Donny asked, shooting Jace a crooked grin. "Jesus drank wine, you know."

"Jesus could handle it. I can't."

"Aw, come on now, pal. You weren't an alkie."

"Don't want to be either. Look, Donny, let's get real here. I haven't seen you in nearly fifteen years. What are you not telling me?"

Donny prowled around the living room, glanced out windows, ran his hands over the backs of chairs, his eyes shifting from side to side as if looking for a place to land. His fidgety behavior elevated Jace's suspicions.

"All right, Jacey boy, here's the straight of it. Looks like you've made a good life in this burg. I figured I'd come down and see what you had working."

Jace snorted. "Me. That's what I have working. Dawn to dark, six days a week in the busy season. I restore historic buildings."

Donny stopped prowling. His shifty gaze focused on Jace. "For real? You're a builder? No side businesses?"

"None."

The admission must have caught him off guard.

Donny grew quiet for a few seconds before the toothy grin stretched wide.

"Okay, I get it now. Ha-ha. I've gone straight, too. Living for Jesus, doing right." With a light laugh, he tapped his chest. "What could be more perfect? You're a builder and I'm in real estate investments. No one knows what we've been through but us. We can help each other, Jacey old pal."

Jace was listening, wanting to believe Donny had changed, but wary. Donny said all the right things, but the tone wasn't quite sincere. He couldn't escape the nagging feeling that Donny was trying to con him. He felt a little ashamed about that, considering they shared a similar past.

"Are you clean?"

Donny fell back, mouth lax, expression hurt. He shoved at his sleeves. "Want to check? Want to see my arms?"

The needle had never been Donny's drug of choice but Jace didn't say so. Instead, he shook his head, the sense of shame deepening. Why couldn't he trust that Donny had changed his destructive ways? Jace had. Why was he so reluctant to believe that someone else could do the same?

"Forget it."

"Hey, no problemo. I was a bad apple. Like you. Two peas in a pod, so to speak. But we've changed, buddy boy. We've changed."

Lord, he hoped so for both their sakes. On the rough streets where he'd grown up boys as young as ten were already using. If not for a good mother who'd begged him to be careful, he'd probably have been a junkie. He'd been bad enough as it was. And Donny knew it.

"I have a sweet deal going in a retirement community in Florida," Donny was saying. "I stand to make money—big money, Jacey boy—and I'm willing to cut you in." He gazed around for effect. "From the looks of this empty place, you could use the extra dough."

Jace's mouth twisted. Donny was still all about working a deal. "Who couldn't?"

"You're interested then? Good."

He didn't say that, but he figured to let Donny talk. Maybe he'd find out what was really going down.

Donny started to prowl again, as restless as a flea. He sniffed, swiped at his nose. "Here's the deal. I sunk everything I had into a couple of investment properties. Then I sold one of them faster than I expected and all my money is still tied up in the other properties. Escrow accounts and all that Housing and Urban Development red tape."

Jace tensed. Now they were getting down to the real reasons for Donny's sudden reappearance in his life. "You came to me for money."

"Buddy, pal, compadre. Listen. You are not hearing me." Donny's voice took on a placating tone as if he was talking to a whiny child. "I came to you because I figured who better to share the wealth? You know me. I know you. We can trust each other."

Like a mouse trusts a tomcat.

"I'm just a little short on cash flow at the present, but the assets are there. I swear to you. On my brand-new Bible." He held up his right hand as though to impress Jace with his sincerity. Jace was not impressed. "As soon as the property closes, I'll be able to pay you back with interest. It's a win-win situation, done all the time in my business."

"Why didn't you go to one of your business associates or to your banker?" Jace crossed his arms again and shook his head. "If you want help ask for it, but give me the facts, not a con."

Donny turned his back and paced some more. Jace could practically see the wheels turning inside his head.

"You should get a couch. One of those long recliner things with the built in tables and cup holders. And a big screen." He stopped, spun. "How do you live in this place without a big screen?" When Jace simply stared at him, he said," This is no con. I swear on my mother."

First the Bible and now his mother. Too much swearing to be true. "I'd like to believe you, but I don't."

Donny stopped his prowling and shoved both hands in his pockets. His shoulders slumped. "All right, look. Here's the real skinny. The economy is killing the real estate business. I've been straight as an arrow for the last ten years, working day and night like you said. Honest. Clean as a new shirt. I swear it. Then the market goes south and I'm struggling. I don't want to go back to that life, Jacey boy. You got to help me out."

Jace suffered a tug of sympathy. He knew the fear of going back, because he lived with it daily. "I'm not rich."

Most of his assets were tied up in this house and the twenty surrounding acres.

"Seeing you on television was like a sign. I'm thinking, go see Jace. He owes you one." Donny stretched out his hands. "I was hoping you would invest in this deal. Just a little to get me going again. After everything that happened, it's the least you can do. I saved your hide, Jacey boy. You'd have died right there if not for me. Torres had you down with no help in sight. No help but me. He was carving you up like a Christmas turkey."

Jace shuddered at the vision of himself on the cold, wet concrete, someone standing on his bleeding hands and Torres with the homemade knife. The scars on his body throbbed.

"One more minute and he'd have cut your liver out and left you to bleed to death. Doesn't that count for anything?"

Jace dragged a hand over his face. It did count for something. "Tell me again where you've been, what you've been doing."

He listened attentively while Donny related his business dealings and his lifestyle among prosperous, law-abiding citizens. Jace wanted to believe he was telling the truth and yet Donny's story seemed inflated to impress.

"You got a second chance at the good life, Jace. Don't I deserve one, too?"

What could he say to that? Donny was right. God *had* blessed him with a second chance and the Lord was no respecter of persons.

"Come on, have a heart. Spot me a few lousy bucks until business picks up."

Jace gnawed the inside of his cheek. He wasn't about to hand any sizable cash to a man he hadn't seen in years.

His conscience pricked. That stranger had saved his life.

"I can loan you a little. Maybe a couple of hundred."

Donny's mouth twisted. "Get real. A couple hundred won't get me to Tulsa."

Jace shifted against the rough lacquered brick, felt the hard pressure against his scarred back and remembered what Donny Babcock had done for him. "What *do* you want, Donny?"

"Well, let's see now." Donny roamed the living room again, looked out the undraped bay window. "I could use a place to stay. A few bucks. Just until this deal goes through. Then I'll be out of your hair. I swear it."

Realization slowly seeped through. Donny was down on his luck and searching for a soft place to land. There was probably no land deal, no money in escrow.

"You're broke."

Donny held up an index finger. A diamond winked from his pinky. "Temporarily short of cash. Emphasis on temporary. I got that deal working."

Jace no more believed him than he could read minds. He blew out a tight breath. He might be a fool, but he couldn't stop thinking about Gary Henderson. What if Gary had turned his back on Jace? Where would he be today?

This one's for you, Gary.

"You can bunk here for a few days."

"I knew I could count on you. Tell you what, old buddy, when I get this deal cooking—"

Jace held up a hand to stop the words. "Listen, Donny, and listen good. No cons. I'm respected in this town. I have a business, friends, a church family. I'd appreciate it if you'd keep a low profile while you're here."

Donny went still. Sly awareness crept across his bony face. "I think I'm getting the picture. They don't know about your little trip up the river, do they?"

Jace shoved his hands in his pockets. "No."

"And you want to keep it that way."

Jace's heart bumped. Not even a town as generous and welcoming as Redemption would do business with him if they knew. "Redemption's a good town. Good people. Don't mess with them. Don't mess with me."

"Well now, the way I see it is this. I got no reason to tell the good folks of Redemption Jace Carter's ugly little secret. No reason at all. You help me out, and I'll return the favor. Get my drift?"

Jace stared into Donny's glittery eyes and felt the earth shift off-kilter. The promise sounded eerily like a threat.

With a heavy heart, he knew he had no choice but to believe Donny Babcock was all he claimed to be. He only hoped that trust didn't cost him everything.

Chapter Four

Two weeks later, Jace listened to the chat and clatter inside the Sugar Shack Bakery while he ate his usual breakfast. He was a regular, preferring Miriam Martinelli's cooking to his own. Other businessmen started their day here as well and he'd learned about more than one restoration job over a plate of bacon and eggs.

This morning he would have liked to sit alone and worry to himself, but the local gathering place was jammed as usual and folks sat wherever they could find a seat.

"Met that friend of yours yesterday, Jace."

The speaker was Tooney Deer, the local mechanic who owned Tooney's Tune-Up. The Native American's chair was crammed between GI Jack and Pop-bottle Jones. Jace and Sloan Hawkins finished out the group of five seated elbow to elbow at a table intended for four. Thick white platters of pancakes, eggs, and meat along with matching cups of steaming coffee crowded the space even more.

Jace stopped chewing. "Donny Babcock?"

Since his arrival, Donny was slippery as a snake. Jace wasn't surprised that he was getting around town. Concerned, but not surprised. He wished every thought about Donny wasn't negative but the man he recalled wasn't worth anyone's confidence. Even though he'd saved Jace from certain death that one time, Donny had double-crossed him a few times, too. And the old Donny Babcock would lie when the truth was easier. The new Donny didn't seem much different.

Jace had offered him a job, primarily to keep an eye on him, but Donny found other things to do. Real labor was never his favorite activity. Like this morning when Jace left the house at six, Donny grumbled something about having business calls to make. Jace was tempted to hang around and see what kind of calls Donny was making, but he had customers waiting.

"Said he's staying at your place for a few days to help you out."

That was Donny. Twist the story to suit his purposes.

"He's here for a few days." He hoped the stay was brief. Since Donny's arrival, he felt as if was holding his breath all the time, looking over his shoulder, waiting for the ax to fall.

"He says the two of you go way back."

"Yeah." To avoid further conversation, Jace bit off a chunk of buttery toast. The last thing he wanted was questions about how and where and when he'd known Donny Babcock. Small town folks with conservative values didn't tolerate criminals.

Just last year the local chief of police had been indicted for murder and sent to prison.

"Nice enough fellar, I guess. Kind of jumpy."

Jace thought the same thing but he'd been alert to any evidence of drugs in the house and hadn't found any.

"Well, lookee here who's coming in the door, looking like Mary Sunshine." GI pointed one of Miriam's fat buttered biscuits toward the bakery's glass door.

Kitty Wainright sailed into the bakery, a soft floral skirt swirling around her legs. Jace's chest clenched. The air in the room seemed to grow lighter, warmer.

Kitty's pale hair fell long and loose this morning with soft bangs framing her small face. If she ever wore makeup, he couldn't tell, but with wide blue eyes and skin like a pearl, she needed no enhancement.

"Mighty handsome woman," GI muttered in Jace's direction before booming, "Howdy, Miss Kitty"

Kitty spun, a ready smile blooming. She raised a hand in greeting. "Good morning."

GI Jack cut his eyes at Jace. "Mmm-hmm. Mighty handsome *single* woman."

Jace shoved in a forkful of scrambled egg and pretended his pulse hadn't kicked into third gear.

"Here's a spot for you, Miss Kitty."

After pocketing two fluffy biscuits and a square pack of jelly, GI Jack pushed back from the table.

"I don't really have time to sit." But she began winding her way through the chairs and tables in their direction.

"Might as well. I'm leaving, too." Tooney took a final slurp of coffee and stood. "That's Pastor Parker bringing in his car right now. Brake job."

Popbottle Jones rose as well, dignity in the old professor's movements. From beneath the table, he retrieved a large canvas bag, the collection sack for his recycling business. "Time and tide waits for no man."

"Yep. Time and tide." GI's head bobbed. "The trash man, too."

The pair of unlikely friends never missed a Dumpster if they could get there before the garbage truck.

Popbottle placed some neatly folded dollar bills beneath his plate and hoisted the canvas bag to his shoulder. The Dumpster divers looked like bums, but Popbottle Jones and GI Jack never failed to tip. "You gents have a blessed day."

In seconds, three men had departed, leaving Jace and Sloan alone at the table. Jace looked at Sloan with chagrin. "What was that all about?"

Sloan grinned. "I think you know."

At that moment Kitty arrived, bringing with her the scent of fresh air and sunshine. Jace's belly knotted in a mix of pleasure and despair. If his friends were matchmaking, they were wasting their time.

Sloan pushed aside a pile of plates to make room for the newcomer. As Kitty settled with feminine grace, Sassy Carlson sailed by, snatched up the plates and swiped a cloth across the tabletop.

"Anything for you, Kitty?" the waitress asked.

"Two dozen doughnuts to go, please. Mixed. When you get a minute."

"Don't say that, you'll be here all day." Sassy's jaunty grin matched her bobbing brown ponytail. "Want some coffee while you wait?"

"Oh, might as well. And one of those decadent sticky rolls that are so bad for me."

"Got it." The waitress sashayed away, dodging chairs, checking tables, and offering comments as she went.

"You're out and about early this morning, Kitty." Sloan casually stirred his coffee.

"The Land Run committee meeting." Clutching a small, flat handbag, Kitty propped her arms on the tabletop. The tiny purse chain clinked against worn Formica. "I'm picking up the doughnuts."

The Land Run Committee was made up of business people and interested citizens who put together all the details of the two-day historical celebration. Jace had never joined the official committee but he helped out where he could.

"Annie and I will be there," Sloan said. "Have you talked to Margo this week?"

Local businesswoman Margo Starks chaired the Land Run Committee along with the mayor. Jace found the woman intimidating but she got the job done.

"Not since the last meeting. Why?"

"She told Annie the vendor list is filling up. The Old West Gunfighters and the trick rider group confirmed."

"Oh, good. Both of those are highlights."

"And…" Sloan paused for effect. "Both groups asked about staying at your motel again."

Kitty clapped her hands. "You're just full of good news this morning, Sloan Hawkins."

"Which means I need to get to those repairs sooner rather than later," Jace said. Kitty needed the extra income that came with the Land Run Celebration but that required all the motel units be in top shape. Which they were not.

Kitty's blue gaze turned on him. "Will you have time?"

"Sure." He'd make time. She was a hero's widow.

His conscience tweaked just the slightest. Dave Wainright wasn't the only reason he found time for the Widow Wainright.

"Will your friend be helping you? He told me about that place in Florida the two of you renovated."

Jace hoped his face didn't register the shock. He'd never been to Florida in his life and to his knowledge Donny knew nothing about building, particularly the special kind of restoration Jace did.

"I can't speak for Donny, but the work will get done in time. Don't worry."

"Oh, I'm not worried. If you tell me you'll do something, you always do." She turned her smile on Sloan. "Redemption's blessed to have someone like Jace."

Sloan cast an amused glance at Jace. "Can't argue that. His expert eye saved me a bundle on Aunt Lydia's chimney. I was going to tear the thing down."

"It's not about the money," Jace said.

"Yeah, yeah, I know. It's the history." Sloan sipped at his coffee, then grinned from Jace to Kitty. "Get him talking about restoration and he's a chatterbox."

Jace grinned sheepishly. Sloan was right. He felt good about making old things new again, and he believed the most dilapidated building could be rehabilitated into something beautiful.

"Why tear down something that's impossible to get back? All that history and character gone forever."

"Which is why Kitty's right. Redemption needs you, my friend."

"I hope you'll still say that after you get my bill."

They all laughed, but Jace reached for his napkin, more for something to do than out of need. Compliments made him nervous. What if he couldn't live up to them? Especially now that Donny was in town.

Kitty leaned forward and, above the smells of coffee and bacon, Jace caught the soft scent of roses. "Which reminds me, I almost forgot to tell you. The closet door in Unit 4 won't close. I know you're busy, but when you get time—"

"I'll run by this afternoon."

Sloan made a funny noise. "Listen, kids," he said. "I'd love to stay—but duty calls. Duty and a gorgeous blonde. Annie and the kids are expecting fresh raisin bread with their breakfasts and I see Hank putting loaves in the case now."

Kitty glanced at the clock above the cash register. "You'd better hurry if you plan to make the Land Run meeting."

"Right." Sloan pushed back and rose, directing his parting remarks to Jace. "Let me know what you think about the attic repair."

Jace nodded. "Call you tonight."

And he was left alone with Kitty.

Jace was on the premises. Again.

Pleasure curled in Kitty's chest. Even from her position in the attic of the laundry room, she could hear his quiet voice talking to someone. He had such a nice voice. Soothing. Kind. She liked to hear Jace talk.

Like yesterday in the Sugar Shack, she'd practically had to pry words from him until she'd asked about the renovations on the old bank and he'd opened up. She'd sat back, nibbled the gooey cinnamon roll and listened to that soothing voice.

Now she could hear it again, somewhere outside the motel units.

She stuck her head through the open hole leading down onto the washer. "Jace!"

The rumbling voices stopped. "Kitty? Where are you?"

"Laundry room."

In seconds, the door opened and sunlight spilled over the washing machine like melting butter. Spring was fully upon them and Kitty reveled in the new awakenings of life. However, spring also meant birds trapped in the attic and she was determined to discourage their nests early on.

"What are you doing up there?" Jace's head was tilted back. He wore an amused expression above his usual neatly pressed jeans and shirt. In one work-gloved hand, he carried a leather tool belt.

Next to him was his friend, Donny Babcock. She'd only met Donny a few times since he'd sat in her office and told her far more about his life than she wanted to know. He was nice enough, she supposed. A little pushy maybe but if Jace liked him, he must be okay.

"Birds." She slapped a hand at a cobweb stuck to her hair. "Phew. I'll need to go through the washer myself when I finish this job."

"Want me to have a look?"

"No, that's all right. I can do it, although I feel bad about destroying all the hard work some poor little pair of birds has done to build a nest. Do you have any extra boards on you? Maybe if I find their entrance points and cover them, the birds can't get in here in the first place."

"Let me come up and have a look." He turned to

Donny. "You can unload the materials over at Unit 7 while I take care of this."

Donny didn't look too happy about the assignment but he flashed a toothy grimace at Kitty and left.

"Come up and I'll show you."

"How did you get up there?"

"The washer."

Jace looked dubious. "No ladder?"

All the blood was starting to run to her head. She must look like a beet by now. A beet with stringy blond hair loaded with cobwebs and insulation.

"Oh, come on, scaredy cat. You can do it."

His mouth curved. "Catch me if I fall?"

Impossible, considering she was above and he was below so she laughed. "Absolutely."

After pocketing his gloves, he handed up his tool belt and stepped upon the washer. When he stood, Kitty's hair grazed his face. He blew it out of the way. And just that simple little connection made her pulse jump. She retreated from the opening.

His hands appeared first, strong and capable. Then as if he was chinning himself in a gym, he pulled his upper body through the opening.

Kitty's pulse fluttered again. For a trim guy, Jace Carter was incredibly strong.

Dust flew around him as he stood. Balancing with booted feet on separate rafters, he placed a fist on either hip. "A ladder would have been easier."

Kitty tossed her hair, laughing at him. "A challenge is good for you."

"I'll remember you said that when we're both in traction."

Kitty laughed again. She felt almost giddy today. It must be spring and the excitement of the coming Land Run Celebration. She glanced at Jace standing there, stance wide, as he stared around at the attic interior. Kitty knew what attraction felt like, though she'd long repressed the emotion out of dedication to Dave. But Annie's comments had her noticing Jace Carter. If she was attracted to him, she didn't want to be, though she had to admit the zip in her blood felt good.

"The birds must be getting in through that vent under the eave," she said, pointing.

"They probably ripped through the screen."

"Can a little bitty bird do that?"

"Sure. Shelter is a powerful incentive."

To prove the fact, wings fluttered around the gap leading to the outside but the bird quickly flew away when Kitty moved in that direction. She picked her way toward the wall, taking care not to step off the rafters. A step down would put her in contact with the ceiling of the laundry room. She doubted the Sheetrock would hold her weight.

"Wouldn't hurt to put a floor up here." Jace stepped gingerly, too, his contractor's eyes studying the wiring as he moved.

"Too expensive. I don't come up here often."

"Once is all it takes."

She wrinkled her nose at him. "Grim reaper."

His mouth curved, and she was tempted to do something else silly just to watch his eyes light up and the corners crinkle with merriment. Sometimes he was too solemn.

"Let's check the nests first, make sure there are no eggs yet."

Kitty caught her lip between her teeth. "What will we do if there are? I don't want to break up someone's happy home."

She expected Jace to tease. Instead, his smile was soft. "Let's look first, then worry."

"Good advice." Kitty started for the closest nest, a bundle of dried grass and twigs.

"Can you reach it?" He started toward her.

She tiptoed. "Maybe."

Straining to see inside the nest, she peeked inside. A wild flap of wings rushed her face. "Oh!"

She jerked back, lost her balance, and fell at an angle across the rafters to slam her shoulder into the side of the house.

Jace was there before the dust cleared. He crouched beside her. "Are you okay?"

A little shaky, she sat up and dusted off her now dirty blouse. "Embarrassed. It was just a bird."

"An unexpected bird. I would have done the same thing."

"Probably not, but you're sweet to say so." She rotated her shoulder.

"Come on, let's get you up and assess the damage."

He took her by the arm, and once again she was aware of the strength in those battered carpenter's hands. Together they stood, Kitty teetering a bit as she sought for balance and to quiet her racing pulse.

Jace hooked an arm around her waist and stood like a solid wall, letting her lean on him, waiting for her to settle. Through the dust of the attic, she caught the scent of soap, aftershave and warm man, scents she'd tried to forget about in the years since Dave's death. A woman missed those manly smells.

"Okay now?" That quiet voice of his soothed something inside her.

Kitty nodded, acutely aware of how close they were, of how solid he was, and of how small and delicate she felt next to him.

Jace cleared his throat and slowly released his hold. She clung to his shoulder a moment longer. "Jace."

He broke contact gently but firmly and stepped back two rafters. His face was tense. "You shouldn't come up here. It's not safe. You're bleeding."

Kitty glanced in surprise at her bloodied palm. "It's only a scrape."

"You should put something on that." He turned his back as though the sight of her blood bothered him. "Go on down. I'll take care of this."

He moved away and went to the damaged vent. Kitty watched his stiff back for a moment longer and then she slid through the attic opening into the laundry room.

Chapter Five

Jace wanted to kick himself.

He finished repairing the attic vents, a simple task once Kitty was safely out of sight. Then he removed the bird nests, relieved to discover that no eggs had been laid in any of them, including the one that had caused Kitty's fall.

He lowered himself into the soap-scented laundry room where the essence of Kitty surrounded him.

She hadn't been hurt, but touching her was reflex. He shouldn't have because now the memory of her velvety skin and rose scent tortured him.

She'd probably thought he was weird the way he'd jerked away like a man on fire.

He rubbed both hands over his face and groaned. For years, he'd worked for Kitty Wainright and been a distant friend. And he'd handled the situation well. Suddenly this spring, keeping his feelings under wraps seemed impossible.

But he had to. Even if Kitty was interested, which she wasn't, he couldn't be.

With a vicious yank of his tool belt, he went in search of Donny.

His boots crunched on the gravel path leading between the motel's cabins where Jace spotted his pickup truck near the target unit. Donny was nowhere in sight.

"Figures," he muttered. He turned to stare at the pretty cottage he knew to be Kitty's home. A fierce protectiveness surged through him. Maybe Donny wasn't over there, but he probably was. Donny always had an eye for ladies and a line a mile long.

Oblivious to the vibrant red and white tulips basking in the sunlight, Jace stalked down the path. Outside Kitty's front entrance, he lifted a whimsical knocker—patriotic, of course, and another reminder of why he had to take care of Kitty but keep his distance, too. He'd set a hard task for himself, but he was determined to see it through. Penance came in many forms, and if his was blond and beautiful with the soul of a saint, he would simply have to cope.

She appeared, still wearing the smudged blouse, though the cobwebs were gone from her silken hair. With her easy smile, she pushed open the door. "Is my attic safe from feathered invaders?"

"Yes, ma'am." Jace removed his cap, held it in both hands like a shield between them. To discourage conversation, he didn't smile. The warm feelings in the attic could not be repeated.

"Is Donny over here?"

Kitty gave him a long, curious look before saying, "He is. Come on in."

Jace followed her slim form into the sunny living area.

The room was small and tidy like its owner, filled with soft, feminine color and dotted with spring flower arrangements. Whimsical figurines of kittens had been set here and there. One brown kitten lay on its back, smiling with abandon. It reminded him of Milo.

"Come on in the kitchen and have some iced tea with us. You must be thirsty after being up in that dirty attic."

He was, but thirst was the least of his problems. He followed her anyway. "I'm sure you have better things to do."

Kitty paused in the kitchen's entry, her expression sweet as honey. "I always have time for friends."

Stab him in the heart and let him bleed. "How's your hand?"

"Oh, that." She raised the palm to display a wide Band-Aid. "I had a splinter. Now that it's gone, I'm good as new."

"Sorry that happened."

"My fault. You warned me." She widened her eyes and curled her lips in a silly gesture that made him smile in spite of his intent to the contrary.

"No traction, though."

She laughed. "There's always a next time."

He hoped not. Neither his heart, nor his resolve, could take it.

Donny Babcock appeared behind Kitty, interrupting the pleasant exchange. Jace didn't know whether to thank him or hit him.

"We have work to do," he said to his supposed helper.

"Why don't you start without me?" Donny flashed his expensive teeth at Kitty. "Kitty and I were getting better acquainted. She invited me to her Bible study."

Something dark and fierce twisted in Jace's belly. "I need your help."

"All right. All right." He gave Kitty a put-upon look and followed Jace out the door.

When he and Donny reached the work area, Jace was still stewing. Part of him worried about Donny's intentions, but mixed up in there somewhere was a heavy dose of old-fashioned jealousy. He shouldn't be jealous, had no right to be, but he was. If Kitty ever decided to let go of her dead husband, she deserved a good man, a man better than either him or Donny Babcock.

He handed Donny a nail puller. "Kitty's a nice woman."

Donny studied the puller as though the tool was an alien spacecraft. "You interested in her?"

"We're friends." He emphasized the word to make a point.

"Good to know. Wouldn't want to nuzzle in on a

friend's sweet spot." He winked. "So you shouldn't mind if I get to know her a little better."

Jace's grip on the hammer tightened. "I do mind."

"But you just said the two of you are only friends."

Teeth tight, Jace pivoted on his toes. "Look, Donny, she's too good for either of us and you know it. Leave her alone."

Donny laughed and propped one hip on a windowsill, the nail puller forgotten. "Just because you want to punish yourself forever doesn't mean I do, Jacey boy. A second chance is a second chance at everything."

Jace tried another direction. Appealing to Donny's conscience wasn't working. As if it ever had. "She's a grieving widow. Didn't you see the motel office?"

"Yeah, a bunch of old junk that needs tossing out if you ask me. A stinkin' shrine to a dead guy. Come on. Get over it."

The callous remark burned Jace. He slammed the hammer into a nail. "Dave Wainright was a hero. He died in service of this country so creeps like us can keep breathing."

Donny pushed off the windowsill, hands spread wide. "Whoa, Jace, you are taking this way too seriously. The dude is dead."

"Kitty is committed to keeping his memory alive."

Donny made a noise halfway between a snort and

a guffaw. "A dead man can't keep her warm on cold nights."

Jace counted to three, took a breath, blew it out. Donny was pushing all the right buttons to bring out the worst in him—a side Jace had hoped was long gone. "I'll say it again. Kitty's a good woman." He leveled Donny with a glare. "Show some respect."

Donny lifted both hands, a gesture he used too often, like some wise guy teenager.

"No disrespect meant, compadre. None at all. Kitty's a free agent. An extremely beautiful one, too, in case you're too hung up on work to notice. And I'm a free man with an eye for beauty."

"She's not interested. You're wasting your time."

"The fun is in the chase, my man. Or have you been a hermit so long you've forgotten?" Donny slapped Jace's shoulder. "Since you got no designs on her, I think I'll take my chances."

After stopping at the plant farm for a flat of geraniums and then at Zinnia's clothing store to look at spring shoes, Kitty walked down the street to the Municipal Building to pay the motel's utility bill. Her operating costs went up while the revenue continued to decline.

She climbed the steep buff-colored steps and entered the dim all-purpose building that housed city hall and other components of the town's government, including the court clerk, city utilities and the jail.

Inside the office marked, "Pay utilities here," Kitty

discovered Cheyenne Rhodes Bowman had arrived first. The pair had become friends when Cheyenne first came to Redemption and stayed at Kitty's motel but they had really bonded in their fight against violence toward women. Since Cheyenne's marriage to the local vet, Trace Bowman, Kitty didn't see her as often as she would have liked. But she was thrilled to see her friend, a victim of unspeakable violence, find fulfillment and joy with Trace and his daughter, Zoey.

"Hey, girl. Fancy meeting you here."

"The utility company gets all of us this time of month." Cheyenne waved the postcardlike bill. "I'm not complaining, though. This is the first bill on the new women's shelter."

Cheyenne had worked tirelessly to buy an older home to turn into a shelter for battered women. Redemption had embraced the project but raising that kind of money had taken a long time. Now the shelter was up and running but with limited space and resources. Most of the services, such as counseling, education and job training came from grants or volunteers. Cheyenne was a whirlwind at securing help for victims, but more money was always needed.

"How's the fundraising going?"

"Slow, but steady. Pray we get the federal grant we applied for. If we do, we'll be able to furnish the other rooms and take in more than one family at a time."

"It's such a great cause. I wish I had more money to invest."

"Things are tight for everyone now. Don't worry. The Lord will supply all our needs according to His riches." Cheyenne grinned, both of them aware that Kitty had led Cheyenne to Christ and taught her some of those key verses as weapons of survival against fear and anxiety. "Speaking of investments, have you talked to that friend of Jace Carter's?"

Kitty blinked. "Donny?"

Black hair swished against Cheyenne's jacket as she nodded. "He came by the clinic the other day and mentioned a real estate investment opportunity that sounded pretty good. Apparently, that's what he does for a living and he's good at it. He made seven figures last year."

"He said that?" Donny dressed well and drove a new car, but seven figures sounded huge, especially to a widow with an old motel falling down around her ears. Every unit needed renovation.

"We were doubters, too, but he showed us the paperwork."

"Really? Interesting. Are you going to invest?"

"Trace and I are discussing it…and praying about it." She handed her check and bill to the clerk across the counter. "Hi Kirsten. This is for the women's shelter."

"Got it. Thanks, Cheyenne."

Kitty took her place at the counter, handing over her payment.

"Gotta run." Cheyenne snapped her wallet shut and slid the slender black leather into her jacket pocket. "Why don't you come to dinner one night this week?"

"I'd like that."

"How's Wednesday? Then we can all go to church together."

"Sounds perfect. I'll be there." She lifted a hand as Cheyenne exited the office, her boot heels tapping lightly on the beige tile flooring.

Kitty took her receipt from the clerk, stuffed it in her handbag and left, too, thinking about investments. Not that she knew too much about them. She had a small savings account from Dave's insurance but the sum didn't draw much interest. Maybe she should talk to Donny.

She stepped out into the bright spring day, her eye drawn to the town square across the street. The pretty parklike area was lush and green and loaded with budding plants. A soft breeze fluttered the American flag waving in the center just beyond the old-fashioned water well that had been hand-dug by the town's founder, Jonas Case, a reformed gunslinger.

Lured by the gorgeous spring day and the little park's peaceful beauty, Kitty crossed to the square. Tiny violets had begun to bloom and their sweet scent drifted on the breeze.

A mother pushing a stroller passed by and Kitty stopped to coo over the baby, a chubby, cherub-faced boy in blue overalls with dark eyes and an easy grin. After the woman rolled on, Kitty turned to watch them go, some hidden portion of her heart opening up to reveal a deep yearning. The what-might-have-beens came to visit. She would have been a good mother if God had seen fit to bless her with a child. Inexplicably, her widowhood weighed on her good mood like a wet, woolen coat.

As she'd learned to do, she allowed herself a minute or two of sadness. Then Kitty closed her eyes and inhaled, letting the park's warmth and fragrances wash away any vestiges of regret. The day was too lovely, and life was too good to spend time looking backward at what could never be. After a cold winter, spring was a gift from God to be embraced.

Cars rumbled past, circling the cul-de-sac that surrounded the town square. She caught the scents of exhaust and from somewhere the smell of hamburgers. Her stomach rumbled a hunger warning. She'd skipped breakfast to run errands and noon was fast approaching.

When she opened her eyes, a white pickup truck turned a corner down the street. She saw a flash of blue on the white door emblazoned with Jace Carter, Restoration and Remodeling. A puzzling emotion leaped in her chest. She stood for a moment longer, staring after the truck in contemplation. She liked Jace a lot, always had. He was easy to be with and she leaned on him quite a bit because of her old motel. He didn't seem to mind. He was simply there when she needed him.

Annie's suggestions had her wondering why.

The memory of their attic adventure surfaced and she found herself smiling.

"Penny for a pretty lady's thoughts."

The voice of Donny Babcock jerked her to awareness. Where had he come from?

"Oh, hello, Donny. I didn't see you come into the square."

"I was passing by and saw you out here, looking lonely. Thought to myself, 'Donny, a beautiful woman like Kitty shouldn't be alone on such a fine day.'"

Kitty wasn't sure what to say. She'd been enjoying her solitary walk.

"I thought you were working with Jace."

Donny frowned and made a dismissing gesture with one hand. "Lunchtime. We'll meet later at the job site. I had business of my own to take care of. Real estate is a demanding venture, you see. People calling all hours of the day wanting to invest. But I'm very particular about who I let in. Shysters are everywhere, looking to make a lot of money off the innocent and inexperienced. Me? I'm a man who protects my investors." He threw his hands up and smiled. "My investors are my friends. People I care about. People I want to prosper along with me. Nothing is too good for them."

Kitty's head spun. Donny was certainly chatty today.

"Have you been to lunch?" He switched gears so fast Kitty's head spun.

"Not yet. I usually eat at home."

"A beautiful woman like you eating alone? On a fine day like this?" He arched back, aghast as though she'd admitted to high treason. Kitty didn't want to be negative, but Donny could be a little over-the-top at times. "No way. You deserve an outing with an admiring man. Have lunch with me. My car is parked in front of the bank." He reached for her arm.

Kitty hesitated. "I really shouldn't."

He pulled a long face. "We need to talk more about Psalm 91. Last evening's Bible study was inspiring but I still have questions. I'm sure a woman of your spiritual depth could help me with them, me being a new believer and all."

She realized she was being railroaded and that Donny's sugarcoated compliments were too much to be sincere, but what harm was lunch? He was new in town. Maybe he was lonely or eager to make friends, and she loved sharing her faith. Maybe she *would* ask him about her investments.

She relaxed her shoulders. "Lunch would be lovely."

Thirty minutes later, over lunch at Bob's Café, Kitty poked a fork at a chicken salad. Donny, it turned out, was a pleasant if somewhat talkative lunch companion. Kitty's mind occasionally wandered to the quiet presence of Jace Carter.

The two men were so different. Kitty could hardly imagine they were close friends. Jace was solid, calm and quiet. Donny seemed almost hyperactive by comparison, and his gift of gab could get tiring pretty fast.

Kitty felt guilty about the last. Donny had asked a dozen questions about the Bible. She should be thankful, not bored.

Several people in the café apparently had already made his acquaintance and stopped by their table to say hello. Donny remembered every name. When Zak Ashford brought up the subject of real estate, Donny offered the firefighter a glossy business card and a wink. "Never mix business and a luncheon date with a beautiful woman."

Kitty stiffened. As soon as Zak left she said, "I don't date."

"What?" Head tilted in bewilderment, Donny slid the gold card holder back into his jacket.

"You called this a lunch date. I'm a widow. I don't date."

"No offense intended. It was just an expression, but really, Kitty, you should rethink this lifetime of widowhood. It isn't healthy." He reached across the table, squeezed and released her fingertips before she could snatch them away. "Your husband loved you madly, I'm sure. He would not want you to be alone forever."

Kitty put her hands in her lap, away from his. "Keeping Dave's memory alive is important to me."

"Of course it is. And you do that very well. You always will." His face twisted with sympathy.

"Moving forward with your life, your *love* life, would be further testament to the depth of your devotion to each other."

"That doesn't make sense."

"I've always heard that people with happy marriages want to recreate that experience. Only those whose relationships were less than ideal avoid romance."

That was the silliest thing she'd ever heard. And if Donny said anything else negative about Dave or their marriage, she would be tempted to rudeness.

"We were very happy," she said, stiffly. "I'm simply not interested in dating again."

Eyes shifting left to right and back again, Donny adjusted his jacket lapel and fidgeted. Apparently, the starch in her spine was showing. "Please forgive me if I overstepped our friendship. We are friends, aren't we?" He offered her a worried smile. "I wouldn't want to be banned from Bible study."

Kitty relented. The mention of Bible study reminded her of why she'd agreed to this luncheon in the first place. "Friends sounds perfect. I'm sorry if I overreacted."

She really was sorry. She normally wasn't this defensive. But she didn't put her hands back on the table.

"I'm the one who has to apologize. I would never purposely do anything to upset you. If I'm disappointed because you won't date, I hope you'll understand. You are a beautiful woman. Any man, me in particular, would find you attractive."

Kitty fought off a blush. Even if he *had* said the word too many times to be sincere, a woman liked being told she was beautiful.

Inexplicably, Jace flashed through her head. Her stomach fluttered. Jace wouldn't throw compliments around like confetti but if he said something he meant it. And it would matter.

The unexpected thought gave her pause. Why was Jace in her head every moment lately?

She patted her mouth with a paper napkin and reached for her purse. It was time to go dig in the flowerpots or paint one of the new ceramic kitten figurines, and get her mind on something else.

"Thank you for lunch. I really need to go. One of my boarders is keeping an eye on the office but I don't want to take advantage."

Donny pushed back from the table and rose, taking the lunch ticket with him. He patted his hip pocket, frowned, then reached inside his jacket. "Oh, no."

"What is it? Did you lose something?"

"My wallet."

"You lost your wallet?" She dipped to search beneath the table.

"I must have left it on the sink this morning." He made a small sound of distress. "This is embarrassing."

Kitty plucked the ticket from his hand. "Don't be silly. I don't mind paying for our lunch."

"Are you sure? I feel like a mooch allowing a beautiful woman to pay for a lunch I invited her to."

Kitty waved him off. "It could happen to anyone."

"Well…" He hesitated only a second before a big smile flashed. "In that case, thank you."

Chapter Six

Jace heard about Kitty's lunch with Donny three times before the day was out. All three times he had to pretend it didn't matter. Kitty was a grown woman able to make her own choices. Even though she seemed fragile to him, she'd been taking care of herself for a long time. He, of all people, had no right to interfere.

He wished she'd chosen anyone but Donny Babcock. There were plenty of single men around and not a one of them with a prison record.

But Donny had paid him fair warning. He was going to make a play for Kitty. It was the play part that worried Jace.

He hooked his tape measure on the lip of Sheetrock and marked the spot where a cabinet was to be built next to a wide bay window. He remeasured for accuracy. His current employers and owners of the Victorian, Alex and Miranda Markova, were perfectionists, but then, so was hc.

"We're thinking about some changes."

Jace refocused his attention on the owner of the house. Worrying about Kitty and Donny was getting him nowhere.

The tape measure zipped shut.

"What do you have in mind?" He was accustomed to clients requesting changes halfway through a project but he was nearly finished with this one. One more cabinet, a few tweaks here and there and he could move on. But the Markovas had the money to do anything they wanted and he wasn't stupid. He needed their business.

"The media room seems too modern-looking." It did to him, too. "Can you redesign the space to incorporate all the electronics and still maintain the Victorian ambience?"

His portion of the media room was already completed to their original specifications. Reworking the design now would set him back a couple of months. But he liked their new idea far better than the current one that didn't fit the house.

After a few seconds of consideration, he grabbed his pad and pencil, always handy, to sketch out a design.

"What about an early 1900s theater look? Maybe like an old opera house? Gilded sconces, mahogany doors, carved molding on the ceiling, maybe murals on the walls?"

Miranda, a small brunette with a store-bought tan and huge earrings, nodded enthusiastically. "Yes.

Exactly." She turned to her husband with a smile. "See? I told you Jace would understand."

"I realize this is outside the original bid." Entrepreneur Alex Markova was as golden blond as his wife was dark, though the tan was just as deep. "We'll renegotiate the contract if you'll draw up some plans for us to look at."

"I can do that. It might take a few days to get the supplies we need. And I have other jobs going that will have to come before the media room."

Mrs. Markova made a small sound of distress but her husband placed a hand on her arm and said, "It'll be worth the wait, darling."

Jace waited for Miranda to agree before saying, "Okay. I'll try to have a rough plan drawn up for you day after tomorrow."

They finished the discussion and Jace gathered his tools to call it a day. Taking on even one more project right now wouldn't be easy. He often hired summer help from the high school shop class but what he really needed was a full-time assistant to learn the trade.

His thoughts turned to Donny Babcock.

Metal clanged against metal as he tossed his tools into the back of the truck. He was juggling three jobs, including the repairs at Kitty's, and now this addition. Donny was living at his house, eating his food—what there was of it—and bumming gas money.

Yet, most times when Jace offered to pay him a fair wage for a day's help, Donny was too busy.

Today was a good example. He'd been too busy to work but not too busy to have lunch with Kitty.

He wondered where Donny was now. At Kitty's? He looked toward town, imagination taking flight.

Acid burned in his gut.

Maybe he should warn her.

He snorted, annoyed at himself. Warn her about what? So far, Donny had done nothing wrong. Jace might not trust the man, but he was jaded. He knew too much. He also knew a person could change.

Donny had a record. Shouldn't she know about that?

If he told her about one, he'd have to include the other. And he didn't want her to know. She trusted him. She might even like him. If she knew what he'd done and where he'd spent three years of his life, her warm blue eyes would look at him with cold distrust.

Indecision warred within. Finally, he came to the only conclusion he could. Keep his mouth shut, the way he'd promised Donny and stay out of Kitty's business.

He squinted toward the west. There was still plenty of daylight left to squeeze in some time at the second job—refurbishing an apothecary museum on Grace Street.

Redemption's street names still made him feel good even after years of driving down the roads and reading the signs. Names such as Grace, Peace, Mercy and Hope had drawn him like magnets when he'd

first arrived. Maybe because he'd needed all of them
so desperately.

Even though he'd deserved nothing, God had given
him a great life here in Redemption.

He cranked the pickup engine and backed out of the
drive. Something rolled in the floorboard and bumped
his boot. One eye to the road, he fished around until
his hand came in contact with a doorknob he'd almost
forgotten. He'd found it in a secondhand shop several
weeks ago. The textured bronze knob was an exact
match for a broken one at Redemption Motel.

He tapped the doorknob against the seat. It was a
good excuse to run by Kitty's, make sure she was all
right, check on Donny's whereabouts.

Before he could examine whether the errand was
for her or him, Jace turned the truck toward town and
the motel.

Trina Wainright was in her late fifties and every
bit as pretty as she'd ever been. With her dark blond
hair and green eyes, she reminded Kitty a lot of Dave.
She'd arrived about ten minutes ago, those cool green
eyes appraising to find Donny Babcock sitting on her
daughter-in-law's living room sofa.

After an initial awkward moment, Kitty had made
the introductions, refusing to feel guilty about having
a friend in her house. Even if that friend was male, it
wasn't as if she was dating him. In fact, she'd tried to
get home from their impromptu lunch without Donny.
Not that he wasn't a nice man. He had to be. He

was Jace's very good friend. But he made her a tad uncomfortable. Maybe the overt friendliness was the problem. Sometimes—too often—Donny assumed a closeness that wasn't there. Once he discovered she'd walked to town that morning, he'd insisted on driving her home. Not wanting to hurt his feelings, she'd reluctantly agreed.

"I found some old photos I thought you might like for the office, honey," Trina was saying as she pulled several eight by tens out of a brown envelope. "I took the liberty of having them copied. If you want, I can get some frames, too."

Stifling an inward sigh, Kitty took the photos and gazed down at Dave when he was a gangly teen with a big, cheesy grin. "They're wonderful. Thank you."

"Mind if I have a look-see?" Donny leaned up, tugging at the knees of his dark slacks to peer over her shoulder.

"This is a photo of Dave." She shifted slightly to one side so he could see and enough to regain her personal space. "My late husband."

"A fine strapping lad. It's very commendable of you ladies to honor him this way." He edged closer, brushing Kitty's shoulder with his. "Very commendable."

Kitty didn't honor Dave's memory to be commendable. She did it out of love. And who said "lad" these days anyway?

Trina's look, frosty when she'd first met Donny, warmed. "Why thank you, Mr. Babcock. It's nice that a friend of Kitty's understands how important it is that Dave not ever be forgotten. That's why Kitty doesn't date, you know. She is fully committed to honoring her vows to Dave."

Kitty heard the emphasis on friend and the less than subtle pressure to keep Donny at arm's length.

"Donny and I just recently met, Trina," she said gently. "He's been attending Bible study." She loved her in-laws. They'd been wonderful to her. In fact, they'd cosigned the loan on this motel so she and Dave could have their dream business. She wouldn't hurt them for anything.

"Oh, well. How wonderful. I'm glad to hear it." Trina glanced between Kitty and Donny and then, as if satisfied with the explanation, returned her attention to the enlarged snapshots of Dave. "Where will you put them? On the shelf or the wall? I'll be happy to help you."

Kitty found her mother-in-law's suspicions laughable. She wasn't attracted to anyone.

That quick, Jace's handsome face flashed through her head. She fought down a guilty blush.

"I'm not sure yet, Trina. The office is already crowded." Most of the photos had come from Trina, hung by Kitty out of respect for Dave's grieving mother. The visual reminders of Dave's life were special to her, too, but she already had plenty. Add the gift shop and the office was jammed to the point of claustrophobia.

The idea caught Kitty off guard. When had she begun to think that?

"Well, I know you'll find a place, honey. You always do." Trina turned toward Donny. "I was telling Chuck before I came over today that we are the luckiest people to have a daughter-in-law like Kitty. Most women would have already forgotten about Dave, but our sweet Kitty keeps the flame burning bright. She even puts fresh flowers on his grave every week." She pressed a finger to the corner of each eye, staunching what Kitty knew were ready tears. "Her devotion means so much to us. You'll just never know."

Guilt and pity warring, Kitty patted her mother-in-law's hand. "I'll find a place for the pictures, Trina."

A knock sounded at the door. Kitty raised a questioning eyebrow in the direction of her guests, shrugged, and went to answer.

When she opened the door, her heart bumped once.

"Jace. Hi." A smile started in her belly and worked its way up to her face. After an afternoon of Donny and Trina, she was inordinately happy to see Jace Carter standing quietly at her door, ball cap shading his eyes.

He held up a doorknob. "I found this."

Kitty blinked, uncomprehending. "Was it lost?"

His mouth curved. "The broken knob in Unit 14. I found this to replace it."

"Oh! Of course. That's great." She stepped back. "Why don't you come in?"

He shook his head. "Better not. Just wanted you to know. I'll fix it now."

"You might as well join us. Donny's here."

Donny's name seemed to be the secret word. Beneath the shady bill cap, Jace's expression shifted. "I don't want to intrude."

"Don't be silly. Friends don't intrude. They belong." She reached out, snagged his still-creased shirtsleeve. "Come in."

"Okay. For a minute." Doorknob clasped in one hand, he stepped around her into the living area.

Donny popped up from the sofa. "Amigo! Qué pasa?"

Jace studied her guest with a solemn gaze. "Donny."

"This is more people than normally attend my Bible study," Kitty joked. "Jace, you know Trina, my mother-in-law."

He removed his cap. "Mrs. Wainright."

"You're the carpenter, aren't you?"

"Yes, ma'am."

"He's a lot more than a carpenter, Trina. He's an absolute building genius. I couldn't keep the motel running without Jace."

"Really?" Trina's green eyes cooled. "That's nice of you. Kitty's husband would appreciate all you do."

"Yes, ma'am." Jace's voice was soft and easy, but the tension in the room had gone up. If Trina was trying to remind them all that Kitty was a widow, she'd done a great job. For the first time ever, Kitty resented her mother-in-law.

"Sit down, Jace. Would you like some tea or something?"

"No, thanks. I should take care of that knob now." He hoisted the replacement in one hand. "Donny, why don't you head out to the house and check on Milo for me? He's probably ready for a trip outside."

"Sure, sure." But Donny made no move to get up.

"Now would be good."

Still Donny didn't budge. Two beats passed while Jace gazed at his friend, and Donny avoided eye contact. Then he nodded to Trina and made his way to the door.

Kitty followed, sorry her mother-in-law had made him uncomfortable and wishing she knew what to say to remedy the situation.

But what *could* she say? She was a widow. And she had vowed never to replace Dave.

Kitty found herself wishing Donny would go and Jace would stay, a thought that troubled her. On the one hand, Donny had been here a long time, but on the other, she would have preferred Jace anyway. They were friends. He was comfortable.

He was also occupying her mind a lot.

She bit her lip. Was there anything wrong with that?

Jace opened the door and stepped outside. The evening sun cast him in a golden light.

"Who's Milo?" she asked, not wanting him to go.

"My dog. A puppy."

"I didn't know you had a dog. What kind?"

"A mutt like me." His mouth curved again. "But cute and smart."

Kitty laughed, tempted to say, "So are you." But she didn't. Trina would choke on her coffee. "I love puppies. Maybe you could bring him over sometime."

"Sure." He stood on the small concrete square of a porch and held her gaze for a heartbeat. Then with his smile lingering and soft, he turned and sauntered away.

Kitty watched him walk across the gravel-covered path until he disappeared inside one of the cabins. A strange yearning pulled at her, a yearning she did not want to name.

Pensively, she shut the door and returned to her guests.

She had some thinking and praying to do about Jace Carter.

To her relief, Donny said goodbye within the next fifteen minutes, leaving her alone with her mother-in-law.

"I should get home myself," Trina said, reaching for an oversize purse. "Chuck will wonder what took me so long."

Kitty figured her mother-in-law had purposely dawdled until the men were gone. "He'll also be wondering where his dinner is."

Both women laughed. "True. He's spoiled. Just like Dave was."

Kitty's look was tender. Even if Trina pressured her about Dave, she loved this dear woman as a second mother. "Good spoiled."

Trina hoisted the big purse onto the crook of her arm. Instead of leaving straightaway, she lingered, apparently something on her mind. Silence stretched until it became uncomfortable. Trina glanced around the living room, her gaze never quite landing anywhere until it returned to Kitty.

"Honey, you know I love you like a daughter. You have been a gift to Chuck and me since Dave's death."

"I love you, too."

"We know that. So please don't be upset when I ask this, but I feel I must."

Kitty tensed. "Ask what?"

"What is going on here?"

"I'm not sure what you mean." She suspected, but she wasn't certain.

"Both of those men are making a play for you."

"Oh, Trina, I hardly know Donny. He's new in town. And Jace…" She wasn't quite sure how to describe Jace.

"Jace Carter has his eye on you. That is as plain as the nose on your face. Why else would he spend so much time on this old motel? You should be very careful. A woman alone needs to protect her reputation."

"Jace is a good man, Trina," Kitty said quietly. "A good Christian man and I don't think you should make assumptions about his intentions."

"Oh." The word was a sound of distress. Trina's hand went to her mouth. "Dave loved you, Kitty. And you loved him. Don't forget that."

How could she ever? "I won't. I couldn't."

Tears swam in Trina's eyes. "Oh, honey, I don't know what I'd do if I lost you, too. Promise me you will never let go of Dave's memory. Promise that Chuck and I will always have you as our daughter-in-law."

Kitty's stomach twisted into knots. She put an arm around her mother-in-law's shoulders and hugged.

"I promise."

The promise weighed heavy on her heart.

A black-and-white police cruiser was parked in front of his house.

Jace's mood went from bad to worse. He thought he'd been stressed when he'd left Kitty's motel, but now the hair rose on his arms. His mouth went dry. And he felt sick to his stomach.

The reaction was unreasonable given he hadn't as much as jaywalked in fourteen years, but he'd never had a cop car in his yard either. Not since he'd moved to Redemption.

He ambled with studied ease down the ten wooden steps of his front porch, Milo dogging his heels. On the bottom step, Milo lost his balance and tumbled headfast, rolling end over end on the new grass.

In spite of his nervousness, Jace laughed.

The cop, who had just slammed out of his cruiser, laughed, too. "Cute pup."

"Yeah."

Jesse Rainmaker climbed the slight incline from the bottom of the driveway to the porch. Jesse, a nice guy in his early forties, had been appointed interim chief of police after the arrest and conviction of the town's longtime chief, Dooley Crawford. Though the shocking event had occurred more than a year ago, the town still chattered about the unexpected charges. No one had ever suspected Crawford of killing Sloan Hawkins's mother years ago.

No one had ever suspected Jace of being a criminal either. He prayed no one did now.

"What's going on, Jesse?" Jace kept his tone casual but his imagination ran wild. Maybe they'd discovered his and Donny's prison records. Or maybe Donny was up to no good and Jace would be implicated. The nightmare would begin again.

Jesse propped one foot on the bottom porch step. Milo sniffed his boot. "Came out to ask you a favor."

A sigh of relief shuddered through Jace. "What can I do for you?"

"There's this kid I've picked up a couple of times, Ned Veech. Vandalism mostly, graffiti." Jesse grinned, teeth white in the smooth Chickasaw face.

"Kid thinks he's an artist, I guess. Wants to spray-paint walls that don't belong to him."

The nerves in Jace's belly tightened. He'd done that. "Not sure what I can do about it."

"Talked to the principal over at the high school. The kid shows up for shop and PE and not much else. Likes to work with his hands. He won't graduate this year, though he should. Not enough credits. I figure if society is fortunate, the kid will get a GED and a job. If not—" Jesse shrugged, the reality of the boy's future obvious.

"This kid got parents?"

"A mama somewhere around. Hard to pin down. Ned's been running loose since he was ten or twelve. Pastor Parker suggested I talk to you. Considering Ned's interest in shop class, maybe you could use some part-time help, be a good influence."

Hadn't he been thinking about taking on help just this afternoon? But not this kind. Not some juvenile delinquent he'd have to watch the way he was trying to watch Donny. Trying and failing. Certainly not some kid who sounded too much like a young Jace Carter.

"I'm not sure I'm the best man for the job." Jace wasn't fit to be anyone's good influence. Besides, he had enough to worry about with his past loitering in his living room.

"Will you think about it?"

What could he say without looking like a complete jerk? "Sure."

"That's all I ask. Just think about. I'll be talking to you." He shook Jace's hand, then leaned down to scuff the top of Milo's head before returning to his cruiser.

Jace watched him go, a heavy feeling in the pit of his stomach. The big city wasn't the only place where a man could find trouble.

He rubbed at his side, felt the rough ridges running beneath his shirt. Every morning he stared at the scars in the mirror. Every morning he remembered who he was and how far he'd come. He also remembered where he never, ever wanted to be again. Gary had advised plastic surgery, but that was one piece of his old mentor's advice Jace had rejected.

There were some things a man shouldn't try to forget.

Chapter Seven

The Land Run Museum didn't fit Jace's image of a historical institution given the concrete and glass structure, but the interior was a restorer's dream. Next to his workshop and his own Queen Anne, the museum was just about his favorite place in Redemption.

With all that was going on in his head lately, he needed to lose himself in the museum for a while and forget the worry of Donny and Kitty, as well as his guilt over not wanting to hire the troubled kid, Ned Veech.

"Maybe you'll find something in this one, Mr. Carter. The entries are early century, right around statehood."

Jace accepted the huge bound volume gently as it was passed to him across a half-moon counter of man-made stone. He always found humor in that. Man-made stone in a historical museum. He used it in plenty of jobs but he still preferred the real thing.

"Thanks, Mrs. Weston. I'll be careful."

"Wouldn't let you look if I thought otherwise." She softened the gruff remark with a wink. Though skinny enough to be blown to Kansas by a gust of Oklahoma wind, the silver-coifed Naomi Weston ran the museum with a stern hand. Because of his work and his interest, Jace was a trusted regular in the museum and therefore allowed into the archives that most visitors saw only from behind glass. That courtesy never failed to warm him from the inside out. It also never failed to ensure his donation to the Friends of the Museum donor drive.

He took the old book to one of the desks set up for research and flipped through the photographs and documentation of early Redemption hoping to find more information about his home as it had appeared in 1906. When he restored a building, he tried to be as historically accurate as possible. Sometimes families had photos. Sometimes old newspapers were a resource. The museum had proven worthwhile time and again.

Maybe he could find something that would make him stop thinking about Kitty Wainright for fifteen minutes.

"Jace, hello!"

His heart threatened to jump out of his chest. With a casualness he didn't feel, he turned toward the sweet, light voice he'd know anywhere. So much for not thinking about her.

"Hi."

"I saw your truck outside. Researching again?"

"As always." Small towns had a way of knowing a person's business. Not that he minded. Not about this anyway. He thanked the Lord the good people of Redemption were clueless about the rest.

Kitty fluttered a hand. "Me, too. The Land Run Committee wants something unique this year. I have no idea what exactly, but I'm looking. Any ideas for us?"

"Can't think of anything offhand, but I'll keep my eye out."

She leaned forward to peer at the book. The scent of roses stirred the air. "Are you researching anything in particular?"

"Mmm," he said, acutely aware of how close she stood. "Anything I can find on my house or the family who first built it."

"You're restoring the old Underwood place, aren't you? The one a little ways from the river?"

"That's it. A three-story Queen Anne."

"I remember that old house when I was younger. Some of the kids thought it was haunted. Those towers *were* kind of spooky. I think kids played in them sometimes."

"And did a lot of damage."

"That's too bad. It must have been really beautiful at one time. The big curved porch and all that lacy trim."

He was pleased she remembered. "Gingerbread

trim. Millwork. It's still there. I just have to bring it back to its glory."

"How long have you been working on it?"

"Three years, off and on."

"And you live there?"

He laughed softly. "Sort of. I live in the part I'm not working on."

He thought of Donny's constant complaints about the dust and the late-night noise as Jace removed walls and replaced windows. A few nights ago when Donny had come in from Kitty's house, he'd griped to the point that Jace had told him the door was open. He could leave anytime. Donny had laughed him off with a remark that still burned in Jace's gut. "Why leave now? I got business bubbling and a pretty woman looking my way."

Jace had pushed for information about the business, warning Donny again not to cause a problem for the town of Redemption. Or for him.

He hoped his houseguest had been listening.

"How much of the house is finished?" Kitty asked.

"Most of the inside, though the upstairs is still a mess. Right now, my table saw is in the master bedroom." At her expression, he chuckled. "I'm not sleeping in there yet."

"Wasn't there an attic and a basement, too?"

"Both. And a carriage house. I'm leaving those until last but the view from the turret's upper window is incredible. You can see all the way to the river."

"Really?"

Her eyes shone with such genuine interest Jace couldn't stop talking. He regaled her with details she couldn't possibly care about—fish scale shingles, spindles and finials—but she kept asking questions, kept smiling encouragement and he just couldn't shut up. He didn't know what had gotten into him.

"Would you mind showing it to me sometime?"

The question took the air from his lungs. "Seriously?"

"Of course, I'm serious. Dave and I once talked about buying a historic house like that." She lifted a shoulder. "Never happened, of course, but I love them."

"You're welcome anytime."

"I'm free Sunday after church."

Jace wasn't sure he could breathe. An afternoon alone with Kitty would be paradise and perdition. And Sunday was about the only time he wasn't working. "Okay."

She shifted on the chair, her skirt whispering as she warmed to the idea. "I have a thought. Near the river is beautiful this time of year. I'll pack a picnic lunch and feed you in exchange for a tour of your castle."

His castle. "I hope you aren't disappointed."

Her smile lit his insides. "I won't be."

Jace turned a page in the book, aware that he hadn't comprehended a thing he'd seen since Kitty's arrival.

Mrs. Weston deposited two more books on the

table in front of him. "One for each of you. Kitty, the old newspapers are still on microfiche. A lot of town photos are in those but this journal of Opal Banks's is filled with town news, gossip, church and school activities. The woman should have been a journalist."

"In a way, I guess she was." Kitty accepted the faded pink embroidered journal and began to read.

Acutely aware of her next to him, Jace had to force himself to concentrate on his own research. He would need months to leaf through all the historical documents archived in the museum but he'd already discovered some old letters from the Queen Anne's former owners. The detail on their daily lives filled him with a sense of belonging. The house they had lived and loved in was now his.

"Jace, look at this." Kitty's voice quivered with excitement. "I think I've found something."

She slid the journal toward him, leaning so they could both see the page. Her shoulder bumped his.

Doing his best to concentrate, though her perfume and nearness filled his brain to capacity, Jace read aloud.

"My heart nearly burst out of my chest tonight, dear diary. Cletus gallantly rescued me from a dreadful fate when a rather seedy man with greased hair—I am most certain he was a gypsy—accosted me in the park. Blanche had gone off to buy ice cream with that flirt Gilbert when it happened. Suddenly, an oaf of a man grabbed me and kissed me! In broad daylight.

Why, I was so distressed, I thought surely I would swoon dead away."

Jace paused to grin at Kitty. She grinned back. "Go on. The good part is coming."

"I thought that *was* the good part." But he read on.

"Gilbert, the handsome swain, took the man to task, demanding an apology which was forthcoming. Then he calmed my near-hysteria with a ride on the carousel. Oh, the delight of the wind in my hair as I reposed on the brilliantly colored horse while Gilbert gallantly held one hand to the brass ring and the other to me. I am delighted the town leaders commissioned the carousel last year. It's the most wonderful addition ever to our beautiful park."

"A carousel, Jace. The park once had a carousel."

"I'd never heard that before."

"Me, either and I've lived here all my life. This is so exciting. I feel as delighted as Opal."

"But hopefully, nowhere near hysteria from being kissed by a most unsuitable gypsy."

Kitty laughed, but Jace wished he'd kept his mouth closed. The image of Kitty being kissed was imprinted on his mind. And the only unsuitable man in the picture was him.

"What if we could find that carousel, Jace? Or one like it? Wouldn't that be a fabulous addition to the Land Run celebration?"

Jace caught her excitement. "It would be, not only

to the celebration but to the park as a permanent fixture."

"Like the one in Central Park! A carousel would draw visitors and raise funds, too."

"The idea is worth discussing with the committee." He hated to be the spoiler but the idea was a long shot. "A carousel won't be cheap."

"What if we could find an old one? I happen to know a terrific restorer." Kitty's blue eyes sparkled.

Certain she meant him, pleasure tickled his chest. He teased, one eyebrow up. "You do?"

"The best, actually. And he's very reasonable."

"His temperament or his prices?"

Kitty's laughter pealed like wind chimes on a warm summer day. "Both actually. Jace, you're too funny."

He was? That was a first. "I wonder what happened to the original? There's always the chance that someone bought it or simply stored it somewhere."

"We can ask around. I'll put an ad in the Register and another online. You never know what might come up on one of those classified ad lists."

"True. I've found some specialty items for my house online."

"There you go then. We can find that carousel, Jace. And if not the original, another. One we can afford." She lit up from the inside out, glowing with excitement.

Jace hated to burst her bubble but practicality demanded it. "We're working under a pretty tight time constraint, Kitty. The Land Run Celebration is not that far away. I think an old carousel would be considered a collector's item. An antique. Trust me, those things are not cheap. Unless we just stumble onto something, the price could be too high. Or the repairs too extensive."

"Which means we need to get right to it." She leaped up from the table, her naturally optimistic personality already churning out ideas. "I'll go to the Register now and then head home to my computer." She wiggled her fingers. "Who knows? I might find us a carousel before dark tonight."

Jace couldn't help grinning at that. "The glass is half-full," he said.

"All the way full, silly. God doesn't do anything halfway."

"You think He's going to help you find a carousel?"

"Well, I wouldn't rule it out."

No, she wouldn't. That was the difference in them, he supposed. One of many. She was the kind of Christian who deserved favors from God.

"I have a few resources I can check."

"Thank you, Jace. I knew I could count on you." She must have been out of her head with excitement because she grabbed both his hands and squeezed. He had the ridiculously high school thought that he'd never wash his hands again.

"We can do this," she said. "I just know it."

Then with energy and excitement radiating from her in waves, she rushed out of the museum.

That was Kitty. Warm, wonderful, and optimistic. He almost believed she could make a carousel appear just because the idea was so good.

She was like a summer breeze dancing through the grass, stirring up an impossible hope that the searing heat would subside.

Jace shook his head and went back to his history, certain the heat in his life might wane but it would always be present to remind him of what could never be.

Sunday morning threatened rain and Kitty went to church with a prayer on her lips. "Please Lord, no rain today."

She wanted to see Jace's house and the work he'd done to renovate the Underwoods' "haunted" house. She also wanted to have a picnic. With Jace. And no, she did not want to examine that desire too closely.

Jace was a friend. She wanted a picnic. And she wanted to talk about the carousel idea. Those were reasons enough to be excited about today and the only reasons she'd suggested it in the first place.

She hoped Trina didn't find out.

A quick glance around the congregation and she spotted Jace, sitting near the front as he always did where he hung on every word Pastor Parker said. Next to him sat Donny Babcock. He'd been attending church regularly and seemed to be sincere in his desire to grow as a Christian.

Yesterday he'd assisted Jace with the roof on Unit 8,

though he'd spent more time in her office than on the job. She'd be dishonest if she said she wasn't flattered by his attention, though she was not attracted to the man. At one point she'd casually mentioned today's picnic, mostly to discourage him. If he'd been jealous, he didn't show it. Over a soda in her kitchen, he'd offered to watch the office this afternoon.

"Kitty." At the stage whisper, Kitty spotted Cheyenne motioning to her. She excused her way past half a row of neighbors and friends to squeeze into a spot beside the Bowman family.

Zoey, Cheyenne's nine-year-old stepdaughter, leaned forward. "You smell good."

"Thank you," Kitty whispered, putting a smile into her words. Though Zoey was blind, she was an amazing little girl who read voices and unspoken moods better than sighted people.

The service commenced with uplifting music and heartfelt worship. Kitty let the stress and worries of the week ebb away. She listened to Pastor Parker's message on the parable of sowing and reaping, and if her gaze wandered to the carpenter near the front, she couldn't help it.

His brown hair was neatly cut in a straight line along the nape. She'd never seen it otherwise, though the cut looked fresh as evidenced by the slight color difference behind his ears. The usual baseball cap was nowhere to be seen and he wore a sage green dress shirt. No tie. She'd have been surprised if he had. Jace was not a tie kind of man though he'd worn one to Sloan and Annie's wedding. Funny that she'd remember such a thing.

His shoulders shifted and the action bunched and unbunched the neck of his shirt. Kitty caught a glimpse of a slender white line running upward from the edge of his collar. Was that a scar?

"Please stand for our dismissal prayer."

Kitty yanked her attention back to the pastor. Everyone had scars. Why were Jace's any more interesting than anyone else's?

After the prayer, Kitty exchanged pleasantries with the other church attendees as she worked her way outside to the parking lot. She had just reached her little red sports car when Jace's voice turned her around.

"Still coming out to my place?"

She nodded. "I thought it might rain."

A grin flashed. "Me, too."

Did that mean he'd hoped it would rain or that he was worried it might? She didn't ask. "But this is Oklahoma. Rain one minute, sunshine the next."

"Don't forget the wind. We always have that." He leaned around her and opened the car door. "You know the way out to the house?"

A frisson of disappointment, totally out of place, filtered through her. She hadn't expected him to pick her up. Would have refused if he'd mentioned it. Why should she be disappointed that he hadn't offered?

"I think I remember, though I haven't been out that far in a long time." She slid onto the upholstered seat, carefully tucking her skirt beneath her. "The picnic basket is packed and ready at home. As soon as I get that and change clothes, I'll head your way. Is that okay?"

"Perfect." He lingered in the space between car and open door. "Sure you want to spend your afternoon in a dusty old house?"

Dusty or not, she wanted to spend the afternoon with him.

The thought rattled her but she managed to say, "Positive. I've looked forward to this all week."

Jace expression was serious. "Then you need to get out more."

Before she could ask what he meant, he pressed the door shut with a snick and stepped away.

Kitty fumbled the key into the ignition, strangely flummoxed, though she wasn't the nervous type. Jace certainly didn't make her nervous.

But he did make her feel something.

Chapter Eight

Jace repositioned the wicker rocker for the third time, then stood on the porch, hands on his hips, to survey his yard. The grass needed mowing. He should have done that yesterday but he'd cleaned a path through the turret instead. Kitty was going to love the view from up there. He'd tightened the railing on the second floor balcony, too, to be sure she wouldn't fall.

"Can't have our first *real* guest tumbling into the rosebushes." He considered Donny as more of a project than a guest. Besides, Donny loathed "this old dump."

Milo, who had trotted merrily along beside Jace as he wandered through the house wishing he had more furniture, now leaped onto the wicker chair, circled once and lay down. When Jace started inside again, Milo immediately leaped to the porch and followed.

"A little sun wouldn't hurt you, buddy." But he held

the door for Milo anyway. The happy creature trotted beside him, ears bouncing. "You think this dress shirt is overkill? Maybe I should change clothes."

Jace shoved both hands up to the back of his head. He should have told her not to come. He should have made an excuse. What had he been thinking in the first place to let Kitty Wainright come out here?

He paced to the undraped window and looked toward the road. Where was she anyway?

Aware he was obsessing, he jogged upstairs, changed into jeans and a work shirt, hung his dress clothes neatly on a hanger, then went into the master bedroom and ripped a few two-by-fours. No point in dressing up. No point in behaving as if Kitty's visit was anything special.

The table saw was in full whine, sawdust flying, when Milo jumped to his feet and sounded the alarm.

Jace's pulse jumped. A look out the window told him Kitty had arrived.

He shut down the machine, removed his safety goggles and knocked the sawdust from his clothes before going to let her in.

Nervous as a fifteen-year-old, he opened the door. And promptly lost his breath.

She'd changed clothes, too. Instead of the silky-looking dress she'd worn to church, Kitty wore a lacy white calf-length skirt with matching white sandals. Her long, pale hair swung freely around her slendcr shoulders. She was like a fairy princess come to life.

"You look pretty." He blurted the words before his brain engaged.

Kitty's smile bloomed. She curtsied playfully. "Why, thank you, kind sir."

His mouth curved. "You would have fit right into the Underwoods' garden parties."

"Oh, no, I wouldn't. I would have been considered risqué. Look at how much of my ankle shows." She lifted a foot. "And these sleeves. Way too much uncovered arm."

The loose, flowing sleeves came past her clbow. "Very improper, Mrs. Wainright."

Kitty laughed and Jace felt the pleasure clear to his toes. Two minutes in her company and his blood hummed and he felt as ampcd up as a speedboat.

"How do you know the Underwoods had garden parties?" she asked. "The museum?"

"Register archives. Leon Underwood owncd thc bank. His wife entertained the social set." It was ridiculous to be so proud of the knowledge, but with Kitty hanging on every word as if he was brilliant, he couldn't shut up. He pointed toward the west lawn. "The fashionable citizens of Redemption played lawn tennis over there."

"And croquet?"

"And probably drank lemonade and gossiped about scandalous women who displayed too much ankle."

His joke was rewarded with another of her glorious

smiles, the kind that lit her small face and widened her bright blue eyes.

"Why Mr. Carter, I had no idea you had such a wicked sense of humor."

Neither did he.

They stood smiling at each other for too long before Jace got himself under control. He'd known this visit would be difficult. Now he knew it would be next to impossible to keep his feelings under wraps. Kitty had only just arrived, and he was already in trouble.

"Better come inside. Maudie Underwood would have been scandalized at leaving a guest on the porch this long."

"I love this porch." But she followed himself inside anyway. "Oh, Jace. Look at this." Kitty pointed up. "What is that called? The stained glass is stunning."

He'd known she would notice, had anticipated her pleasure. "It's a transom. Some called it a fanlight because of the shape."

"The peacock's colors are brilliant. It can't be original."

"I think it is. I found it in the basement with a lot of other old windows and doors. Some things were in decent shape so I've used them throughout the house. This piece of stained glass was probably my favorite discovery. I had to replace the frame. I couldn't believe the peacock was still intact."

"Unreal. I love it. It's incredible."

Milo, waiting impatiently to be noticed, stood up on his back legs and yipped.

"Well, hello." Kitty turned her attention to the puppy. "Aren't you a cutie?"

Milo spun in excited circles.

"This little nuisance is my best buddy. Milo, say hello, and mind your manners."

Kitty crouched down and scooped the pup against her cheek. Her skirt pooled around her feet. "What a precious baby."

She stroked his ears and chest and crooned in a sugary voice. Milo flopped to his back, tongue lolling, eyes closed in unmitigated delight.

"He will now love you forever and there's not much you can do to discourage him."

"Love is always welcome," she said airily. Then as if she'd said something out of turn, she blushed and turned away.

Jace, too, got caught on the word love. He believed in love. Maybe even hungered for it, though he wasn't about to let himself go there. He figured Kitty was flustered because she felt the same.

Still carrying Milo, she stepped from the foyer into the living room. Jace struggled against embarrassment, worried she'd judge him lacking because the rooms were mostly empty. He shouldn't care but he did.

"Not much furniture yet. Sorry."

"Let me guess. You're looking for certain pieces and won't settle for less."

There she went again, saying exactly the right thing. "Something like that."

"Is this mantel original?" With Milo happily adorning one shoulder, she ran the opposite hand over the richly polished red oak.

"Rebuilt from the original."

She raised an eyebrow. "By you."

The words were a statement, and Jace found a certain gratification in her unspoken vote of confidence.

"Painstakingly. I took weeks to get it right."

"This is incredible work. You've been wasting your time working on that motel of mine." She moved to the bay window. "This, too?"

"Mostly restored. Some of the wood was rotted and replaced."

"You have amazing talent. Amazing."

Funny how a compliment could light him up inside. He was confident in his work, knew he was good, but having Kitty acknowledge the ability validated him somehow. "I don't know if I'd call it talent or persistence."

"You'd need both to be this good." She slid onto the window seat and faced him. The light from the uncovered bay window enveloped her. Milo wiggled, gave a puppy groan. She moved him to her lap where he settled with a sigh. "I can visualize a young Victorian woman here, reclining on a lace or velvet pillow as she stares out the window, writing in her diary or awaiting her beau." She pressed a hand to her heart and fluttered her lashes dramatically. "A suitable young swain drives up in his father's two-horse rig and escorts her to the park where an *un*suitable gypsy very well might kiss her."

Jace's smiled widened. If he wasn't careful, his face would break from grinning at every little thing she said. "You're a romantic."

Her eyes widened in playfulness. "Does it show?"

"Just a little." Enough that he wondered how it would feel to be a normal man, a man with the freedom to be a romantic, too. "Come on, I'll give you a tour of the rest."

"So impatient," Kitty teased. "You must be getting hungry."

Imitating her, Jace widened his eyes and blinked rapidly. "Does it show?"

Laughter spurted from them both. He couldn't remember when he'd felt this young and playful.

He'd been old since he was eighteen.

After exploring the other downstairs rooms Jace hesitated. "Upstairs is dusty and messy. You sure you want to go up?"

"Don't back out now, Jace Carter. You promised a view from the attic turret."

"Ah, yes." He rubbed his palms together. "The Tower of London."

"Eek!" She ran squealing up the staircase with Milo bobbing against her shoulder.

Tickled by her reaction, Jace trotted up behind her.

Milo raised a lazy eyebrow as if to say, *"Don't you wish you were me?"*

Yeah, he did. Lucky dog.

At the top of the stairs, Kitty stopped to admire the gleaming wood balusters. "Fancy. I can see lots of work went into refinishing all this scrollwork."

She had no idea how right she was.

"The result is worth the effort."

"I won't argue that. This staircase is magnificent. Are you going to put carpet on the steps?"

"Haven't decided. What do you think?"

"Mmm." She gave the matter some thought. "I don't know. Probably. Otherwise the house will echo. And I like my creature comforts."

He'd planned to leave the stairs natural, but now he was rethinking. Cold floors weren't his favorite either.

They reached the second floor and rounded the landing. He'd cleaned most of the rooms as well as he could, but sawdust covered the master bedroom and bath.

"Sorry about the mess."

Kitty waved him off as she gazed around the disheveled space. Besides the table saw, the floor was littered with various tools, a box of nails, a five-gallon plastic bucket, and a wad of drop cloths.

"This may be an odd question but where do you sleep?"

He grinned and spread his arms. "Anywhere I want to. I have an air bed. There's a finished bathroom downstairs, too. The master bath is through there. I went for modern conveniences instead of Victorian reality."

She peeked inside. "The claw tub is fabulous."

"Refinished. Not by me, though. I hired a pro. Everything else is modern."

"But it still feels historical. I like that."

"Me, too. I gutted the walls pretty much everywhere and redesigned the floor plan to suit today's lifestyle. But I couldn't give up the old doors and windows, the crown molding, the woodwork. It's too rare and beautiful to destroy."

"This house wouldn't be the same without it. You're doing an amazing job." She spun slowly in a circle, blue eyes taking in every detail in a way that said her interest was real. "I imagine the Underwoods would approve."

"I hope so." But *her* approval felt pretty sweet.

They wandered on through the other empty, unpainted rooms. Jace was acutely aware of Kitty at his side, of the way she murmured appreciation for the workmanship and gasped with delight at the geometric surprises and the stunning detail in the old house. He asked and she offered her opinion of paint colors.

"I never thought about using red."

"Not red, Jace. Black cherry."

"I stand corrected. Black cherry." He stroked his chin in thought, visualizing the alcove with white glossy trim and deep red walls. "Could work."

"It will. I know my colors. You'll love it. And you'll have to invite me back so I can say I told you so. Now when do I see this famous turret?"

He pointed upward toward the attic. "No time like the present."

"Is it creepy?"

He couldn't resist. "Yep."

"Ooh, cool. I love creepy."

Jace's lips curved. She was so cute.

In one of the many nooks of the second floor was a door to the attic staircase. Jace turned the knob. The area inside was dark and the smell was dank with old wood. He flipped the light switch. "I've not done any work up here other than rewiring. It's dirty."

"Will you stop apologizing? I'm washable." With a flounce to her step, she headed up the narrow steps. Milo, still hanging over her shoulder, bobbed contentedly along. Relaxed and drowsy, he looked more like a shoulder stole than a living creature.

"A servant must have lived up here," Kitty mused when they reached the top. The floors were in place and a wall to either side of the stairs divided the space into rooms.

"Maybe someone's barking mad relatives. I warned you. Tower of London."

Kitty gave a pretend shiver and giggled. "How Gothic of you, Mr. Cart—Oh!" The single word was a cross between a gasp and sigh. "Look at this. Oh, Jace. The view."

She was across the space and into the octagonal-shaped turret in a matter of steps. A semicircle of tall windows washed clean by Jace's persistent hand rose from weathered wainscoting.

"Like it?" He already knew she did. Like a child gazing into a candy store, she pressed her face close to the panes.

"Magnificent. So green and vast and—look at the carriage house." She pointed a finger.

The carriage house, now a garage with storage overhead, mimicked the design of the big house. "I've not done any work out there either."

"But it's so pretty. Like a colorful doll's house, only bigger. Did you plant the flowers?"

Jace followed the direction of her point. "Nah, those come back every year. They're old and deep. Maybe even planted by Maudie Underwood. Maybe by a servant. I'm not much of a gardener. I don't even know what most of them are."

"Well, then, you need my expert horticulture services. I happen to be an avid gardener, as you can probably tell by the constant digging around my house." She pointed, drawing his gaze downward. "See that stunning coral bush? Japonica. And the tiny purple flowers? Hyacinths. They're lovely little things with a soft, sweet smell."

So was she.

She swiveled her face his direction. Her shoulder brushed his. Jace's disobedient heart bumped.

"I can give you some pointers if you'd like. The

backyard is too pretty not to garden. Have you thought about adding a gazebo?"

Her voice was eager, stirring him to agreement. But he was already in over his head, both with work and with her. Self-preservation kicked in. "No time right now."

"Oh, well, maybe later."

He'd noticed the motel's pots and window boxes she kept filled with red, white and blue flowers and the bushes growing neatly besides each cabin. She loved gardening.

"I appreciate the offer."

"Anytime. Really, Jace. I mean that. You've done a lot for me. I'd love to putter around in your gardens."

He could see the tiny starbursts in her blue eyes and the curl of her eyelashes. Warmth ebbed from her skin to his.

Try as he might he couldn't look away.

He swallowed, fighting down a vicious urge to touch her cheek. "Keeping the motel in good shape is my job."

Her blue, blue eyes searched his. Jace realized they'd both turned and now faced each other, barely a breath apart.

"Why, Jace?" A tiny pucker appeared between her eyebrows. He wanted to smooth it away and make her smile again. "Why do you play handyman for a beat-up old motel when you're clearly overqualified and overworked?"

GI Jack and Sloan had both asked him the same question.

"Your husband's a war hero. I respect that."

Something stirred behind her eyes before she turned back to the window. Pink stained the tops of her cheeks. The urge to brush his fingertips across the warmed skin was strong in him, but he was a man with great discipline. Discipline he'd learned the hard way.

Kitty grew quiet and Jace didn't know if he'd upset her or simply reminded them both of who she was.

He wasn't about to forget who he was.

"Is that a pond in the distance?" Her cheeks were still pink but she seemed determined to move the conversation forward.

He shouldn't have invited her here.

"A big pond. In the mornings a mist rises and hangs over the water. Deer and other animals come to drink. It's pretty."

She made a small chuffing sound. "An understatement, I'm sure. Do you come up here to have your coffee? I would if this place was mine."

Don't go there.

"Sometimes I do. Sunrises are spectacular. I saw a turkey yesterday. Maybe I'll buy some ducks if the coyotes will leave them alone. The Underwoods' daughter, Susannah, kept ducks. Kind of a novelty, I guess because the family used the pond as recreation. They fished, swam, canoed." Some mornings he imagined them there, in nineteenth century garb, enjoying nature in a way most people today didn't take the time for. "There's still the remnant of an old rope swing. Probably not theirs but I like to think so."

Her mouth curved and she angled toward him again. "You know a lot about the Underwoods."

"This was their dream home. Now it's mine. I like knowing about them. I like thinking of the lives they led here and that they might be pleased with what I've done. Whenever I restore a section or read one of their letters, I feel...a connection, I suppose." Embarrassed, he huffed and glanced away. "I guess that sounds silly."

He was talking too much. When had he gotten so wordy?

Kitty shook her head, and the gorgeous hair he longed to touch swished against the curve of her face. "Not silly at all. I'd call this a labor of love. I understand about those."

Softly, he said, "I guess you do."

She touched his shirtsleeve. "You're the keeper of their memories."

He was. And she was the keeper of a hero's memory.

Jace took a step back. Kitty's hand fell away and she stood watching him with an expression he could not comprehend. He shouldn't have invited her here. He'd known it would be torture. Having her here only made matters worse.

Lord, help me. I'm in love with her.

It was the first time he'd ever allowed himself the full thought, though the emotion had been hovering in his heart for years.

He felt idiotic, helpless, hopeless.

He focused on the distant, shining body of water and beyond to the narrow line he knew to be Redemption River.

A man had drowned there a few weeks ago. "We should head back down."

One hand holding Milo steady, Kitty said, "You must be starving."

"I could use a bite." And more space between the two of us.

"Me, too." She stepped away from the window but lingered in the oddly-shaped room for a few more minutes while he stood like a helpless teenager watching and yearning. She skimmed delicate fingertips over the wide window trim and the ancient paneling. She took in the rough planked flooring, the swags of cobwebs hanging overhead, the thick grime of age and unuse.

"I love this room, Jace. I've never seen anything like it. If I lived in here, I would turn this space into something I could use every day. It's far too wonderful to be hidden away in an attic."

Her innocent phrasing caught in his brain and spun in repeating circles.

If she lived in this house—an impossible thought he'd never get out of his head now that he'd seen her here.

If she lived in this house.

He'd loved this place since he'd first seen it, the porch sagging and half the windows broken. Now he wondered why he'd bought it. What good was a huge family home to a man who would never have a family to share it?

Chapter Nine

Kitty smoothed the corner of the red tablecloth for the third time.

"Might as well give up. The wind will win."

Jace sat across from her, a soda can dangled over one raised knee. The wind ruffled the top of his hair and the sunlight shot golden highlights through the brown. He was such good company, easy to be with, easy to talk to. All through their picnic lunch of roast beef sandwiches they'd talked, moving easily from topic to topic. She'd enjoyed this outing every bit as much as she'd anticipated.

"I am a tenacious soul." She plopped the wicker basket onto the corner, opened the container and dug inside. "Want another cookie?"

He accepted the offered treat just as he'd eaten every other thing she'd pulled from the basket. His appetite was gratifying to a woman with no one to cook for. "I don't get home baked cookies very often."

"I bake them more than I should." He knew that. He'd even brought her a kitty cat cookie jar after the third or fourth time she'd plied him with a zippered bag of snicker doodles and chocolate macaroons. She'd never thought the gift unusual until lately.

"It doesn't show." He took a man-size bite of the fat chocolate chip cookie.

"I pawn most of them off on my tenants and anyone else who comes around."

"Like me." His hazel eyes twinkled.

She raised one shoulder. "I like to bake. I like to eat. And I like to give them away. You and Donny are both willing victims of my cookie baking mania."

"Donny, too, huh?" Jace shifted position. "Is he bothering you?"

"Who? Donny? No, no. He's very...nice." He was nice. Too obvious maybe, but nice enough.

"Good." He didn't seem convinced.

"Is there some reason you're asking?"

He shook his head but his eyes didn't meet hers. "Just wondering."

"He really has been nice to me, Jace, if you're worrying that he hasn't. A few days ago, he helped clean the flower bed around the vacancy sign. Before that he offered to change the oil in my car. Tooney does that so I said no, but he was thoughtful to offer."

"You like him then?"

"Well, sure. I guess so. He *is* your friend. That's pretty high recommendation."

"Look, Kitty, I   " He started to say something more then shook his head. "Never mind."

"What? Is there something I should know? You're starting to worry me." Kitty thought back to the moment in the attic when she'd wondered if she'd upset Jace. He'd spun away and left so quickly. But once out of the turret, he was himself again. He had that same look again, as though he held something back. As Annie said, still waters run deep and Jace was about the deepest man she knew.

"Donny and I knew each other a long time ago, Kitty. I hadn't seen him in years until he showed up here. I don't really know him that well anymore."

Oh, that was all. "Do you think he's changed?"

The question seemed to trouble him. "I don't know."

"I've only seen and heard good things, Jace. I'm sure you don't have to worry. A lot of people like him, even my mother-in-law who is suspicious of every single man under the age of sixty." She laughed softly.

"Can't blame her." The corners of his eyes crinkled. "Men are suspicious creatures. Even that one."

He nodded toward Milo. The dog sprawled next to him, belly up to the sun, pink tongue hanging from the corner of his mouth in total relaxation. She'd never seen a puppy so confident in humans. Jace must be a kind and gentle master.

He also had a gentle sense of humor she really liked. There was a playfulness in Jace Carter that he kept under wraps most of the time. In fact, there was a lot to this man that he seemed to keep under tight control. She wondered if he'd always been this way or if something had happened that forced him inside. And if someone had wounded him, was that person a woman?

Funny that she'd wonder such a thing.

"Why aren't you married?" As soon as Kitty blurted the half-formed question, heat flooded her neck and face. "I'm sorry. That was rude. I don't know what's wrong with me."

"Don't worry about it." He reached into the basket for another cookie. "These are great."

So he didn't want to answer. Which probably meant there *had* been a woman. Now her curiosity was fully aroused. Was he pining for a woman who had jilted him? Was that why he didn't date? She knew for a fact he didn't, because Annie and Cheyenne had mentioned it over and over again.

Oh, this was ridiculous. She couldn't believe she was even thinking such things. Jace's love life, or lack thereof, was no business of hers.

She dusted the crumbs from her skirt. "Let's walk down to the pond."

Though the original plan had been a picnic by the river, once here, Kitty hadn't wanted to leave Jace's property. It was that beautiful. They'd opted for a spot in the vast green backyard beneath a pair of giant oaks.

Holding the cookie between his teeth, Jace pushed to a stand and reached out a hand. "You'll like it."

Kitty slid her fingers into his and was not surprised when the calloused grip was strong and firm. She *was* surprised at the ripple of warm pleasure that ran through her at his touch. When was the last time she'd held a man's hand even for something as mundane as this? When he started to let go, she tightened her hold.

He stilled and shot her a questioning look. Feeling playful and happy, Kitty tugged and unbalanced him. He stumbled two steps before catching himself.

He laughed. "Strong woman."

"Don't ever forget it either, mister." She flexed the other arm, winning a wide-eyed look of mock fear for the effort.

Happiness bubbled up and flowed out as laughter.

Later, she'd beat herself up, but right now, she was enjoying the company of a man she liked and respected. And she refused to feel guilty about it.

Trina would have a fit.

Guilt tried to push in and spoil her day. She didn't want to hurt her in-laws but they would not understand her friendship with Jace.

Her stomach tightened, tamping down the glow of giddiness. Was she starting to feel something more for Jace than simple friendship?

Jace figured he should drown himself in the pond and get it over with because right now, holding Kitty's small hand in his was about the nicest thing he'd done in a long time. Try as he might, he couldn't make himself let go.

They strolled, hands swinging playfully between them like little kids, across the big backyard and past the carriage house. Kitty's pretty white skirt swirled around her legs in the spring breeze and Milo darted in circles, startling at butterflies and wind-ruffled grass. Kitty giggled.

"He's so funny."

"Yeah. Milo's a trip. I like him."

She turned a happy face toward him. "Me, too."

He was powerfully tempted to pull her close to his side, to slide an arm around her waist.

"Any progress on finding a carousel?" He didn't give a five-cent nail about the carousel at the moment. He just wanted to stand in the sunlight and look at Kitty's heart-shaped face and marvel at her bluer than blue eyes.

She shook her head. The wind captured the long locks of hair and set them dancing. "Not yet. But the committee is thrilled with the idea, too. And," she said dramatically, "I have some leads."

"Yeah?"

"I asked Ida June. She's one of the oldest people in Redemption but her memory is razor sharp, especially about things that happened years ago."

"What did she say?"

"The original carousel was removed when she was a little girl. She thinks it was stored somewhere. Oh,

Jace, if we could find the original. Wouldn't that be something?" Her face lit up with excitement.

"Sure would be, considering that new ones are out of budget and the antique carousels are unbelievably expensive. Like vintage cars."

"Any responses to your internet search?"

"Nothing solid, but I have hope." Not a lot but he wasn't going to rain on her parade.

"Same here. If we can just make contact with someone who knows exactly where the Redemption carousel was taken…"

"Maybe we should talk to Popbottle Jones and GI Jack. Not much slips past those two."

"That's a good idea."

"Don't know why I didn't think of them before. I'll stop by tomorrow after work."

"Where are you working now?"

"Samuel Case's antique store, the Markovas' Victorian up the river a ways and the old bank building on Main."

"Not busy, are we?" she teased. "Donny should help you more."

"I don't think he's much into building."

"Really? I thought he was an expert."

Jace bit his tongue to keep it still. The only thing Donny was expert at was lying. He'd never helped Jace build or renovate anything until he arrived in Redemption. And the work he'd accomplished so far could have been done in a half day. "I guess he got tired of it."

"You should hire an assistant. With the economy like it is, I'm sure there are plenty of men who could use the work."

"I'm giving the idea some thought." And a lot of prayer. "I need someone with training but there's this kid. Chief Rainmaker and the preacher think I should hire him."

"Who is it?"

"Ned Veech. You know him?"

"Ned? Yes. Anyway, I used to. He was a cute little boy, shaggy reddish hair and big brown eyes. He rode the church van to Sunday school when I taught the junior class."

Jace screwed up his forehead. "I don't remember him."

"He didn't attend very long. His family never came either. I prayed a lot for that child. He said some things in class that made me wonder if the home was troubled."

"From what Jessie said, the kid is starting to get into trouble now. The chief thought working with me would help. Seems Ned likes shop class. Had some crazy idea that I would be a good example. A mentor, or some such." He rolled his eyes and snorted. The idea was ridiculous.

Kitty squeezed his fingers. "Don't laugh. You would be. Maybe the Lord sent Jessie to talk to you because you are exactly what Ned needs."

"I doubt that." The Lord would know better. Jace wasn't what anyone needed. Yet, he hadn't been able to get the kid off his mind. Was that the Lord giving him a push?

"You could use an assistant, even someone to do your gofer work. Think about it, Jace. Ned was a sweet child and if he's leaning toward trouble, he needs a Christian man's influence. What could it hurt to try?"

What if he failed? What if the kid got worse? What if Ned did damage to one of the work projects? Didn't Jace have enough to worry about with Donny hanging over his head like a noose?

His conscience poked at him. What if Gary had never offered Jace a hand up? Where would he be now?

All right, Lord, I'm hearing you loud and clear. I don't like it, but I hear. "I'll talk to Jessie."

Kitty's beam of approval made the decision easier to swallow.

They neared the pond, a silvery-topped body of water, shaded on one side by native pecan trees and sunny on the other. An aluminum boat lay on its belly on the shore.

A huge white bird flapped to a landing on the far side. Tall, skinny legs waded silently into the shallow water. Jace tugged Kitty to a stop and whispered, "Shh. Look."

A small, pleased gasp escaped her. She pulled her hand away and clasped it against her mouth. Jace figured the break in contact was for the best, though the cool air rushing in against his hand was not nearly as pleasant as the feel of Kitty's warm skin. He'd had no business touching Kitty in the first place but when she'd clung to him, he'd not had the good sense to resist.

He didn't know why she'd held on to him that way. His insides had gone a little crazy. She hadn't known, of course. And she'd meant nothing by it, he was certain. She had no idea how he felt about her. If she knew, she'd run away so fast, the tailwind would cause a tornado.

Kitty had spent seven years mourning a husband. She wasn't about to stop now. Jace had always felt safe in her company because of that dedication to Dave's memory. There was no chance of her getting the wrong idea about his intentions. He was her handyman. End of story.

This afternoon had rattled that assumption.

"Is he fishing?" Kitty whispered, rapt focus on the great white heron.

"Yes. He's good at it, too. I've watched him before."

While they whispered, the heron's black bill shot below the water and emerged with a shiny, wiggling fish.

Kitty squeaked. "That was fast!"

Milo let out a yip and bolted toward the pond. The startled heron lifted off with a great flap of wings.

A laugh spread inside Jace's chest. "Milo has a way with the birds."

"Squirrels, too?"

"How'd you guess?"

Milo reached the water's edge and slammed on his brakes, skidding on the wet bank. He teetered for a moment, then backed away and stood gazing at his reflection with a worried expression.

Kitty laughed. "That was close. Can he swim?"

"I don't know. He hasn't been brave enough to try."

About that time, Milo lunged awkwardly into the shallows. Water splashed as short legs began a frantic dog paddle. Milo's little head bobbed up, ears flopping back, his eyes wide with panic.

Kitty gripped Jace's shirt sleeve. "Jace, he's going to drown. Do something."

Though he seriously doubted the dog would drown, Kitty's distress was as real as Milo's. Jace broke into a jog and reached the bank in seconds. As he stretched toward the flailing animal, he had a quick flash of the day at the river when his reach had not been enough to save a drowning man.

He snagged the pup and lifted him out of the water. Milo burrowed into Jace's neck, trembling. He clasped the dog to his chest, affection welling for his little buddy.

"Dumb pup."

"Poor Milo." Kitty had reached the pond's edge and her fingers stroked the pup's soggy fur. "Is he okay?"

"He would have been fine if I'd left him alone. Dogs can swim." He lifted Milo from his soaked shoulder and set him on the ground. The pup shook himself hard, slinging drops everywhere. "Sorry."

Kitty waved the apology away. "As long as he's all right."

"He is. Embarrassed maybe but not hurt."

Milo flopped over on his back and wagged his body back and forth on the grass. Jace grinned, amused. He reached down and picked up a pebble. "Ever skip rocks?"

"I'm a small-town girl. Of course I have." She rubbed both hands together. "Show me what you got."

He let fly with a nice sidearm and watched the stone bounce five times before going under.

"Pretty good. Now, let me try. Friends and I used to do this out on the river." She reached for her own rock and sent it sailing. It hit the water with a *glunk* and disappeared. Kitty made a cute face. "I was bad at it then, too."

Though he tried to hold back, a snort burst from Jace's throat.

Kitty spun toward him, face merry. "Stop! You're laughing at me."

"No, I'm not. I'm laughing with you."

The ridiculous statement tickled her, too. She thumped him on the shoulder. "Meanie."

"Here, let me show you how it's done. Skipping rocks is like riding a bike. It'll come back to you." Holding a flat stone sideways between his thumb and finger, he showed her the technique. "The trick is in the wrist. Flick your wrist like you would a Frisbee."

He handed her the stone.

"Like this?" she asked.

"Looks good. Feet apart, side turned toward the water, hunker down a little and let 'er rip."

Kitty's face was a study of concentration as she followed his direction and tossed the rock out over the gently rippling water. Again, the stone dived straight under.

Jace bit his lip to hide the grin.

Kitty turned toward him, hands spread wide, eyes daring him to laugh.

"I never could ride a bike, either," she groused.

Laughter burst from Jace's throat. Kitty was so much fun to be with.

"Blame the instructor."

"But I *can* ride in a boat. Are you going to row me around or not?"

"You want to?"

"Well, yes. Wouldn't Maudie Underwood expect it?"

"I suppose she would." He knew he was getting in over his head. A boat ride on a private pond was personal, romantic even, but he could no more refuse her wish than Milo could hoist an oar.

Against his better judgment, Jace righted the small craft and was amused when Kitty added her diminutive weight to push the boat into the pond.

Jace held the bow close to the bank while she

stepped inside, then tossed the oars in and started to join her.

"What about Milo?"

The pup, having rolled in the grass and shaken himself numerous times, rushed toward them but put on the brakes when he saw the water.

"I'm not sure he's seaworthy," Jace said, amused. "He looks nervous."

Milo responded with a pitiful whine.

"How can you resist that? I'll take care of him."

Jace scooped up the dog and handed him in, then climbed in, too.

"No more swims for you," Kitty crooned as she stroked the puppy's damp head. Milo, the schmoozer, gazed at her with adoration. Jace knew exactly how he felt.

With an oar against the bank, he pushed off, and slowly circled the craft toward open water. With Kitty sitting next to him on the bench, his moving arms grazed her. She didn't complain. Neither did he.

"Did the boat come with the house?"

"No. I bought it."

"To fish in?"

"Mostly I row around and relax. Ever looked at the moon and stars from a boat?"

"No, but I'd like to sometime."

He shouldn't have asked. The image of gliding these peaceful waters in the darkness with Kitty was too vivid. He could picture her lying back, face rapt in the moonlight as they counted stars together. He would touch her face, listen to her soft breathing and her sweet voice. And he would kiss her.

A deep yearning nearly pulled him in two. He had no business thinking that way, no business dreaming the impossible. He was a marked man, a broken vessel that God had somehow glued back together. He tried hard to be a decent Christian, but nothing he could do would ever erase three years in Lexington Prison.

"Whatsoever a man soweth, that shall he also reap."

The scripture was carved into his spirit like the scars on his body. He'd heard and read them often during his years in the pen and he knew them to be true. He'd sown bad seed and now he had to reap the consequences. As long as Kitty didn't know the truth, at least he could be her friend. And he could watch out for her. Even though she'd been married and now ran a business, she was sweet and innocent and believed the best in people.

There were always sharks in the waters looking for the vulnerable.

Donny's face came to mind and Jace prayed that he hadn't been responsible for bringing a shark into Kitty's life.

He took up the oars and stroked the water easily, letting the work burn away the stress gathering in his shoulders like a dark enemy.

Kitty trailed her fingertips in the water. Once, she flicked him with droplets and he growled in playful response. She talked, about the white flowers growing along the pond dam and the tiny tadpoles darting through the shallows.

Jace listened, relishing the sound of her voice and the soft splash of oar against water. She asked questions about his work and he told her about the Markovas' theater room and a secret passage he'd once found in a house.

"How fascinating. I wonder what it was for?"

"Bootlegging probably."

"Couldn't the house have been on the Underground Railroad?"

He paused in rowing. "Did they have that here?"

She shrugged. "Probably not. Oklahoma wasn't even a state during the Civil War."

"I still vote for bootleggers."

"Or outlaws. Like the house in Kansas where the Dalton Gang had a secret tunnel in and out. Redemption is known for attracting outlaws."

Jace's blood chilled. He kept his voice light and his face averted. "Plenty of those in the 1890s."

"True. Plenty here, too, I'm sure. Men who came to outrun their pasts but the past wasn't far behind. They'd have to have a hiding place or an escape route."

Jace didn't know what to answer so he kept quiet, something he hadn't been able to do all day. With her easy acceptance and sweet spirit, Kitty drew him out of his usual reserve.

They floated along, content to say nothing for a while. Soon the sun began to fade and long shadows fell across the water. The spring air cooled. Kitty shivered.

"Cold?"

"A little." She rubbed her arms. "I really should go home."

She didn't sound enthusiastic. Jace didn't want to be happy about that but he was.

"It will be dark soon."

"I've really enjoyed today."

So had he, but he kept the enthusiasm to himself.

He rowed to the bank and leaped out to secure the boat, then pulled the nose onto land. Milo hopped to the ground with a quick shake. Kitty stood, wobbling, and Jace reached out to steady her. One hand on his forearm, she placed the other on his shoulder. Without thinking, he grasped her narrow waist and lifted her easily to shore. His arms were strong from constant work and she was light as air.

"There you go." He didn't release her and she didn't step away.

Like frog song, the evening air pulsated around them. Blood rushed in Jace's ears like a windstorm. He held on, though common sense said to release her. She was ashore now and steady on her feet. She wouldn't fall.

"This has been…wonderful," she said, her voice barely a murmur.

"For me, too." Maybe the best day of his life. Certainly one of them.

He wanted to ask her to come back again. He

wanted to tug her close and hold her, maybe even kiss her. Instead he gazed into trusting blue eyes and knew he didn't deserve her trust. He was a lie she didn't know about.

"Jace?"

He swallowed, throat thick. "Yeah?"

Her small fingers dug gently into his shoulder. If she moved them an inch, she would feel the ridges of his scars.

"I never expected to want to spend time with a man other than Dave."

God help him.

"You should go." Unable to trust himself another minute, he dropped his hands from her waist and started off toward the house. "I'll walk you to your car."

Chapter Ten

Kitty felt like a fool. What has she been thinking? A romantic ride in a boat and she'd practically thrown herself at Jace. And he'd rejected her.

What had come over her? She didn't date. She didn't even flirt. She was committed to her husband.

A husband who was gone.

At the voice in her head, tears sprang to Kitty's eyes. She slashed angrily at them. Dave was dead. And she had promised to honor his memory all the days of her life.

But she really liked Jace Carter.

Obviously, he did not return the sentiment.

On her knees in the flower bed next to the cottage, she yanked at a wad of crabgrass, pulled it up by the roots, and slammed the tenacious weed into the bucket at her side.

She was lonely. That was all. And Jace was a nice guy kind enough not to take advantage of a pathetic widow.

Yet for a minute there, she'd felt…something. She didn't know. All last night she'd tossed and turned, confused and upset. This morning, she'd awakened exhausted and cranky.

Most likely she'd misread Jace's signals. It had been a long, long time since she'd been out on a date.

Not that yesterday had been a date.

She yanked another weed and slammed it into the plastic bucket.

"Weeds do have a way of frustratin' a fella."

She jerked her head up to find GI Jack standing not two feet away. Dressed like a bum and unshaven, gray sprigs shooting from beneath a disreputable ball cap, he was a frightful sight. Good thing she knew and trusted him or she'd run screaming.

Next to GI, his equally disheveled business partner, Popbottle Jones, studied her with interest.

"Oh," she said, embarrassed at having been caught in a fit of temper. "Good morning."

"Is it?"

She sat back on her heels, one wrist resting on the bucket rim. Weeds and dirt spread around her like battle carnage. She *had* been having a fit.

"This is the day the Lord hath made. I will rejoice and be glad in it." Her forced smile was nothing short of hypocrisy.

"Indeed," Popbottle tilted his long neck to one side. "Yet, I detect an uncharacteristically disgruntled undercurrent in your normally blithe demeanor. Is something amiss?"

"I'm fine. Really. How are you two this morning?"

Before either could answer, the rumble of an approaching pickup truck drew their attention. They glanced toward the end of the drive and the approaching truck. Shading her eyes with a forearm, Kitty rose to her knees.

The truck pulled to a stop and a familiar-looking young man hopped out. Kitty recognized him from the lumberyard.

A slammed door disturbed the quiet.

"Ms. Wainright? We're here to replace that bad ceiling. Jace Carter sent me."

"Jace? But I thought he—" She stopped when Pop-bottle and GI both turned speculative gazes on her. "Unit 8." She motioned in the general direction. "The door's open."

"Right." The young man's face was pleasant. "I'll get you fixed right up."

Kitty watched him go, an odd dissatisfaction taking root in her belly. Why had Jace sent someone in his place?

"Brought you a little something, Miss Kitty," GI Jack said.

"You did?"

She shouldn't have been surprised. GI Jack was a junk artist and she'd been the happy recipient of his work before.

"Well, you see, I save things. I reckon you know that. All kinds of beautiful buttons and gewgaws get throwed away." His grizzled old head bobbed up and down. "Yep. Sure enough. A shame, too."

"What my friend is trying to say, dear lady, is that you've been our topic of conversation of late."

Kitty rose from her spot next to the peonies and peeled off her gardening gloves. When she flapped them against her thigh, soft, moist dirt pattered to the ground. "I have?"

GI's head bobbed again. "Yep. Yep. Sure have. On our hearts. And with that inspiration, I made something."

He delved into his jacket pocket and removed a small object wrapped in a plastic shopping bag. The sack crinkled as he opened it.

"There you go. See? It's a little trinket box." He held it toward her. "I'm told ladies like those. This'n is a heart. A broken heart, put back together with things nobody else wanted. Castoffs. Uh-huh. That's the way of it."

"Oh, GI Jack, it's beautiful." Touched, Kitty took the trinket box and stroked her fingers over the heart-shaped lid, made from some sort of metal, carefully shaped and painted in pink hues. It was covered with a conglomeration of colorful buttons, beads, shells and shiny objects arranged in eye-pleasing order. GI had the gift of creating beauty from chaos.

In a departure from the normal lift-off lid, this one opened in the center where two halves of a jagged heart met and joined perfectly. She raised the delicate pieces.

"There's an inscription. Just for you." GI's thick finger poked at the bottom of the six-inch box. "Right there."

"She can see it, GI."

Indeed she could. In perfect engraving, done she suspected by the artist himself, was a scripture.

"Revelation 21:4." She looked up. "I don't know that one."

"Reckon you'll have to look it up, then, won't you now?" GI Jack seemed delighted by that turn of events.

"Or you can tell me."

"Maybe Popbottle can. He's better at memorizing than me." Like a child, GI urged his friend. "You want to tell her, Popbottle?"

The old professor shook his head. "Some things are better read and pondered."

GI Jack offered his usual head bob. "True. Read and ponder, Miss Kitty. And be blessed."

Curiosity rose in her. Knowing these two, the verse in Revelation had special meaning. But what? And why?

"I think I'll go in and get my Bible. Would you gentlemen like to come inside, too, and have some tea?" To GI Jack she said, "I have raspberry lemon."

GI smacked his lips. "Sounds mighty promising, Miss Kitty, but we got rounds to make."

"A rain check perhaps?" Popbottle asked.

"Anytime." Kitty smiled. The two old roamers had lightened her mood. "Thank you again for the gift."

"You are more than welcome. Now, you run along and look that up." After what seemed to be synchronized nods, the two old men sauntered off down the gravel path toward the main street.

Kitty pressed the box to her heart and watched them go, wondering.

The loading dock of the lumberyard was a busy concern on Monday morning. A dozen contractors and general citizens were lined up awaiting materials.

"We can deliver this on site, Jace."

"I'll haul it. You're pretty busy this morning."

The foreman, Doug Stastny, nodded his shaggy blond head and began sliding stacks of mahogany onto Jace's truck bed. The material had arrived for the Markova house. At least someone would be happy this morning.

Jace removed his hat and rubbed the back of his hand over his forehead. "Hot already."

"And getting hotter." Sweat running down the sides of his face, Doug cast a cynical eye toward the west. "It'll probably storm."

The phrase was common in Oklahoma. A warm, windy spring brought storms.

"Hope not. I have outside work later today." Rain brought delays to construction sites and he could not afford any more delays.

"Pretty fancy wood for Kitty's motel," the foreman commented. Wood slid against wood and over the metal bed to thud against the cab.

At Kitty's name, Jace flinched. He hadn't slept more than two hours last night and when he had fallen asleep he'd dreamed of Kitty. The dream was sweet and wonderful—like her. He'd awakened with the smell of her perfume in his head and a heart as heavy as his truck.

Last night's incident at the pond could not happen again. Nothing had actually happened, but it could have. He'd spent all evening beating himself up over it. How did a man control both his brain and his heart at the same time?

"The mahogany's for the Markova job." Coward that he was, he'd subcontracted today's repairs on the motel. He wanted them done, wanted Kitty to have everything she needed, but he didn't have to be the one doing them.

"Where's that helper of yours?"

Jace bit back a sigh. "Not helping me, that's for sure."

The foreman laughed. His Slavic cheekbones cut sharp angles beneath his eyes. "Didn't seem the type."

Didn't Jace know it? Donny came and went at will without telling him a thing. Not that he had to, but his actions added to Jace's concerns.

He'd been nowhere around when Jace had awakened this morning. To his knowledge, Donny hadn't come home at all last night. After firing up the coffeepot, Jace had gone into the future study where Donny slept. A pile of dirty clothes said his houseguest was still in residence but there was no sign of him. Jace hadn't seen him in three days.

His gut told him Donny was up to something. He hated that he couldn't believe the man had changed. He'd even prayed for a better attitude, but so far, the attitude grew worse. And finding Donny gone again this morning had deepened the worry.

He'd glanced around the room for clues to Donny's activities, afraid he'd find drugs or paraphernalia, but he'd seen nothing out of the ordinary. A few papers here and there, a brochure for a resort in Florida, a notepad. Curious, he'd looked at the writing and frowned to see Trina Wainright's name and phone number.

He still wondered what that was all about. Considering Trina's she-wolf attitude, he wasn't going to pry.

But thinking of Trina brought him right back to Kitty. He'd promised to work on the motel. He'd also promised to look for the carousel. He could do the latter from a distance.

"There you go, buddy. All loaded." Doug slapped a hand against the side of the truck.

Jace hoisted a gallon of lacquer and then slammed the tailgate. "Doug, you've lived around here a long time."

"All my life."

"Did you ever hear of a carousel in the park?" He'd been asking everyone that question.

Doug rubbed his chin. "Seems I recall something. Why?"

"The Land Run Committee was interested in it."

"Did you ask Popbottle Jones? He's a pretty good historian."

If the carousel still existed, Popbottle Jones and GI Jack could have seen it on their recycling excursions.

"He's on my list. Thanks, Doug." He slammed into his truck and headed toward the Markova house. The carousel would have to wait until after work.

At seven o'clock that evening, after a particularly hard day, Jace lifted the shoe-knocker on GI Jack's unpainted front porch and waited for the expected oogah-horn doorbell to announce his presence.

A pair of dogs lazing on each end of the porch barely lifted an eyelid. The real power around here wasn't the dogs. It was the goat. Braced for a head butt from Petunia, he was glad when GI Jack opened the door before the goat arrived.

"Get in here, Jace Carter. Missed you at the Sugar Shack this morning."

"Off to work early."

"You're hungry then. Come on in and have some cheese."

Hiding a smile at the unique refreshment, Jace followed the man through a living space crowded with boxes and bags and piles of everything from computer motherboards to broken dolls. A chandelier of colored bottles hung from the ceiling and cast a pleasant stained-glass glow over the mess.

"What brings you out our way this p.m.? Wouldn't be wanting to renovate this fine house, now, would you?" GI Jack chuckled at his own joke as he shuffled to the refrigerator and took out a large, cloth-covered round of white goat cheese.

Jace slid onto a tall stool drawn up to a long, low bar. For all the junk piled in boxes and stacked into corners, the kitchen was relatively neat. He wasn't too worried about getting poisoned, anyway.

"My schedule's a little tight right now. I could work you in next year."

They both snorted. Anyone who knew GI Jack and Popbottle Jones also knew the home filled with Dumpster treasures was exactly the way they wanted it.

GI picked up a butcher knife the size of a hammer and sliced off a fat chunk of cheese. "There you go. Petunia's finest. Folks in cities pay a big price for that, you know. Got some crackers over here somewhere, too. Ah, here we go."

Jace accepted a pair of crackers, loaded them with cheese and took a bite. His stomach was empty from skipping lunch and the soft crumbly cheese and salty crackers filled a void. "Tell Petunia I appreciate this."

"She heard you." GI nodded toward something behind Jace's back. He swiveled around to see Petunia sauntering in from another room.

"Thanks, Petunia."

She bleated softly and gave him a gentle head butt.

"She likes you, Jace Carter, and she is a fine judge of character."

"She probably likes Hannibal Lecter, too."

"Ha." GI Jack chortled. "Good one."

Jace popped the rest of the cracker into his mouth, chewed and swallowed. "Did you ever hear about a carousel in the park?"

"In Redemption?"

"Back at the turn of the century. *Last* century."

"Well, let's see." GI Jack rubbed the back of his neck and stared up at the ceiling. "I recollect something, but Popbottle is the memory keeper. He's the one to ask. I just make stuff."

GI Jack's art was more than "stuff." "Is Popbottle around?"

"Yep." He shuffled to the back door, cupped a hand around his mouth and yelled, "Popbottle, we got company."

In less than a minute, the old professor came huffing through the door.

"Jace here is asking about an old carousel. The one used to be in the park. You know anything about it?" GI Jack slid Jace another cracker with cheese and lifted an eyebrow toward Popbottle who shook his head against the offer.

"There was one. Why?"

Jace repeated the story from the Land Run Committee, conveniently leaving Kitty's name out of the mix, though he had no illusions that he would be searching for the carousel if anyone else was looking for it.

"We had this idea that a carousel in the park, like the one in Central Park, could make money for the town. Since the old carousel is part of the town's history, we thought it would be a nice addition to the Land Run Celebration."

"We? I didn't know you'd joined the committee."

Jace sidestepped. "The idea was mentioned to me in case we found one that needed restoring."

"Ah." Professor Jones nodded sagely. "I see. And would the person who mentioned this happen to be Kitty Wainright?"

Wily character. "It was."

"Ah," Popbottle said.

"Ah." GI Jack wagged his head up and down in agreement. "Mmm-hmm."

Jace shifted uncomfortably on the bar stool. He hadn't come here for one of their amateur psychotherapy sessions. "So do you know anything about the carousel?"

"Might." With a dignity belying his ill-fitting black jacket and baggy brown pants, Popbottle Jones pulled out a bar stool and climbed up beside Jace. "Is something afoot between you and the lovely widow?"

"Not a chance." Plastic rattled in the quiet as Jace reached for another cracker. Petunia head-butted his elbow, demanding a bite.

"Well, that's too bad. She's interested."

Jace gulped. The cracker stuck in his throat. He coughed. "In me?"

Both old men cackled.

"No, in one of us," Popbottle answered. "Wake up and smell the roses, son. They don't bloom forever."

Jace didn't know what to say. Only he knew why Kitty was off-limits. Finally, he mumbled the one thing that was true and unchangeable. "She's out of my league."

"Time for a fine woman like that to stop mourning the dead and start living again."

Jace was tempted to cut and run. He didn't need this today. Yesterday with Kitty was too fresh and sweet, and his heart was still messing with his mind. "I repair her motel."

"Broken hearts needed fixing, too. We figure you're the man for the job."

"You're wrong about that." Jace pushed off the bar stool. "Thanks for the cheese. I gotta go."

"Running away never solved anything."

Yes, it did. It had. "You boys have the wrong idea. Kitty and I are friends. I work for her. That's all."

"All right, all right. I get the message. Mind my own business. I'm not too good at that most of the time."

GI Jack chortled as Popbottle Jones slid off the bar stool to follow Jace to the door. Jace couldn't get there fast enough. He was on the porch and headed for his truck in seconds flat.

"About that carousel."

The carousel turned Jace around. "Yes?"

"The city took it down in the forties to recycle the metal for the war effort. Many metal things were sacrificed back then. Tractors, signs, gum foil. You name it."

"The horses and most of the structure would have been wooden. Any idea what happened to those?"

"As I recall, a number of residents complained bitterly about losing the carousel so the demolition crew stored the leftovers in the city barn."

Hope leaped. "You think they might still be there?"

Popbottle's jowls quivered with the head wag. "The barn burned to the ground in the sixties."

Jace's heart sank and with it the hope of finding the carousel for Kitty. His online efforts thus far had been limited. "Back to the drawing board."

He pivoted, hands shoved in his pants' pockets in disappointment, and headed to the truck.

"Not so fast, son." Popbottle Jones strode toward the truck, a spring in his step. "You didn't let me finish."

Jace opened the truck door and slid onto the bench seat. When he glanced up Popbottle stood not three feet away, staring at him with wise eyes.

"This search of yours. It's not really about the carousel, is it?"

Jace stared at the wise old Dumpster diver. Every cell in his body wanted to blurt out the truth, to ask advice, to lean on someone other than himself. But a secret told was no longer a secret.

When Jace didn't answer, Popbottle said, "Nothing wrong with falling in love with Kitty Wainright. No use denying such a fine emotion, son."

Jace clenched his hands on the steering wheel. He didn't dispute the statement because he couldn't.

Popbottle Jones' fleshy cheeks wrinkled in a smile. "Well now, when a man loves a woman and wants to please her, he does things for her that no other man would think of doing. Things like hunting down an old carousel when he's so busy with his own work he has no time to eat or sleep. That's how a woman knows he loves her."

"I have no right," Jace muttered, mostly to himself, but Popbottle Jones was there and he heard.

"A man can't always control his heart. Now, his head, that's a different matter. Sometimes you have to stop thinking so much. Anyone can see Kitty's eyes light up when you're around. And everyone in town knows you're in love with her. Have been for a long time."

Jace suppressed a groan. "She's a widow."

Popbottle Jones bristled. His voice took on professor's stern, admonishing tone. "Dave Wainright wasn't the selfish type. Both of you need to stop using him for an excuse. It's disrespectful."

The notion jarred him. Disrespectful?

"Being afraid to venture out into the deep river of emotional attachment is one thing. Using Dave as an excuse is another. Far as I can see, there's no reason for a good man and a good woman not to be together if they want to be."

That was the problem. He wasn't a good man.

"*Is* there a reason, Jace Carter?"

Jace met the old man's steady, probing gaze, blood hammering in his temples. With a heavy sigh, he nodded. "Yes. There is."

The professor studied him with sympathy. "I thought so. A good reason, too, I suspect?"

Jace dragged a hand over his face. "A real good reason."

And that's all he was going to admit.

"You've prayed about it, I suppose?"

"Plenty." He'd prayed not to do anything stupid. He'd prayed for God's forgiveness. He'd prayed not to love her. Was that what Popbottle meant?

"All right then. I won't pry." The statement made Jace smile despite his discomfort. Popbottle Jones and GI Jack were notorious for prying. "But if you need a sounding board, I'm available. I've never shared a confidence in my life."

"I appreciate the offer."

Popbottle tapped lightly on the rearview mirror and stepped back from the truck. "Last I heard Carver Case had that old carousel."

Jace blinked to clear his head, his dread changing to hope. "Carver? Simmy John's dad?"

"I suppose Simmy John has it now that Carver's passed."

Jace didn't know what to say. He'd gone from hope to disappointment to worry and now back to hope. He could never be the man Kitty Wainright deserved but if he could find the carousel, he could give her that.

With a nod, he slid the shifter into reverse. "Thanks, Popbottle."

"A tree is known by the fruit it bears, Jace Carter."

And with that cryptic statement, the old professor turned and walked away.

Chapter Eleven

"Don't you think that's strange, even for Popbottle Jones and GI Jack?"

Kitty sat on the tan sofa of her friend, Cheyenne Bowman, a Bible opened on her lap, the trinket box next to her.

Face serious, the darkly pretty Cheyenne cocked her head to one side. Kitty could practically see the wheels turning inside Cheyenne's sharply intelligent mind.

"Read it again."

Since receiving the trinket box from GI Jack, Kitty had read the scripture from Revelations a dozen times.

"And God shall wipe away all tears from their eyes; and there shall be no more death, neither sorrow, nor crying, neither shall there be any more pain: for the former things are passed away."

"Why would they give me a verse about the resurrection?"

"Did it ever occur to you that they're trying to tell you something?"

"Well, yes, but what? I know about the end-time promises."

Cheyenne made a face. "Which is still a lot more than I know. Maybe your theology is getting in your way. Maybe these verses mean what they say, and they're talking about the here and now, not the sweet bye and bye."

Kitty furrowed her brow and said softly, "You think they're telling me to stop grieving for Dave."

Compassion filled Cheyenne's face. "We all think that, Kitty. All your friends. You are young, beautiful and smart. You have so much life in you. It seems tragic that you choose to be locked in the past with death."

Tears sprang to Kitty's eyes. "It's not like that. I loved him, Cheyenne. Dave was the other half of me."

"I know. I know." Her friend leaned in for a side hug. "But Trace loved Pamela, too. They had a child together and he was every bit the devastated husband when she died. Where would I be if he was still clinging to her memory?"

With Trace's love and patience, Cheyenne had come out of a deep, dark struggle of her own. Come out stronger, happier and married to Trace, the man who refused to let her suffer alone. Theirs was a love story everyone in Redemption liked to tell.

"Trace was ready. I'm not."

"Aren't you? You told me yourself you were tired of being alone every night. That's why you started the Bible study."

Kitty clenched and unclenched her clasped hands. The thin paper of the Bible crinkled beneath the movement. Could Cheyenne be right?

"I can't just forget about Dave."

"No one's asking you to. You can honor and remember Dave and still have your own life. Read that passage again and think about it."

Kitty smoothed the rumpled pages and read the words again. When she finished, she sat staring into space, thinking. Was this a message from the Lord? Or was she letting selfishness in the form of feelings for Jace push Dave into the background?

"I don't know, Cheyenne. I've lived so long holding Dave's memory up for the world to admire. I'm not sure I know how *not* to do that. I'm even less certain it's the right thing to do."

"I think the Lord is telling you that the past is over. Stop mourning and start moving forward, and he will dry your tears just as he did mine."

Kitty still marveled at the transformation in Cheyenne from a fearful woman shattered by violence to a joyful Christian wife free from anxiety and bitterness. But Kitty wasn't like Cheyenne. She wasn't broken. She was a healthy, happy woman who'd lost a beloved husband to war.

Kitty squeezed her temples with finger and thumb.

"It's very confusing. Dave's mother puts a lot of pressure on me. She'd be devastated."

"Kitty, listen to yourself. Is the memorial to Dave for yourself, for Dave, or for his parents?"

"I don't know." Confused, she rubbed the ache tapping at the side of her head. For seven years, her life had had one focus. Changing that focus was scary.

Cheyenne gave her leg a single, solid pat. "Think about it. Pray about it. Do what's right for you. If you're happy and content where you are, then don't let any of us well-meaning friends change your mind. But if you're not...well, it wouldn't hurt to test the waters. There are plenty of single men in Redemption looking your way."

Kitty gave a short laugh. "I wouldn't say there were plenty."

Cheyenne pushed a long strand of black hair over her shoulder. "I can think of one in particular."

"I don't think so, Cheyenne." She had until yesterday. "If you're talking about Jace, I think he is exactly what he claims—a good man who believes in caring for the widows and orphans like the Bible says. That's the only reason he comes around."

And she had a sad feeling he wouldn't be coming around much anymore.

One look at Ned Veech and Jace saw trouble with a capital *T.*

Body cocked to one side in the universal sign of teenage contempt, the surly youth couldn't look any more disinterested in training with Jace Carter. Standing in the anteroom of the high school counselor's office, Ned's hands were jammed deep into his pockets, his lips tight and slanted, his nostrils flared. Reddish-brown hair was parted on the side and hung low over one eye. The other, uncovered eye glared at the world with dark brown fury.

Jace offered up a prayer for guidance and fought back an urge to walk out. Gary had probably wanted to walk out on him more times than he could count. But his mentor had stuck. Lord, help him do the same.

"I can use you if you're willing to work."

The boy didn't respond.

"Your shop teacher says you're good."

That stirred him a little. "I am."

And Jace knew it for a fact. He'd taken the time to look. Ned had raw talent and an eye for the unique. If Jace was going to repair and restore the carousel, he needed to hone and harvest Ned's skill and do it fast.

He was still thanking the Lord and marveling that he'd found the carousel at all. Just as Popbottle Jones had said, the carnival ride had been stored in the far reaches of Carver Case's cavernous shed beneath a tarp and a pile of other junk. Simmy John had forgotten it was even there until Jace asked him. Now, the carousel was in Jace's workshop, sorely in need of a face-lift.

"Want to prove it?" he asked the surly teenager. "Earn some cash in the process?"

The one brown eye flickered. "How much?"

Jace named a price above minimum wage. "If you're really good, that goes up."

Ned straightened just enough that Jace could read the signals. "I'll quit school for that kind of money."

"Stay in school or the deal is off."

The teen shrugged. "I'm not going to graduate anyway."

"So graduate next year."

"I don't know."

Jace knew better than to coddle a kid like Ned. Any show of weakness in the early stages of a relationship would mark Jace as weak. Kids like Ned needed a leader, not a mama-figure. He knew because he'd been this kid, and his sweet mama hadn't been able to do a thing with him.

If Ned didn't grab hold of something positive fast, he'd soon be dealing drugs or robbing houses. If he wasn't already.

"Suit yourself. It's your funeral." Jace spun on his boots and started out of the counselor's office.

His hand was on the doorknob when he felt Ned move. He could hear the thoughts shifting like sand through the teen's head. He expected Jace to come back, to try to convince him. But Jace didn't hesitate. He yanked the door open with a loud rattle and stepped out into the hall.

He didn't need the attitude, and yet an excitement had started to build inside him the moment the shop teacher showed him a wooden mask Ned had designed and built. The thing was creepy, like something from an African death dance, but it was good. Really good. The kid wasn't interested in traditional building. He was interested in crafting art from wood.

What was a traditional carousel except wooden art?

Jace was halfway down the tall steps leading into Redemption High School when he heard Ned coming. Still, he didn't look back. The bar lock popped as the door was slammed open. Footsteps hustled over the concrete.

"Hey!"

Jace hid the grin building up in his chest. He paused, but didn't turn around. Let the kid come to him.

One, two, three, four fast steps. "Mr. Puckett said you're building a carousel."

"I am."

"I can do it." There was a suppressed undertone of excitement in Ned's voice. Jace understood. He got excited about new projects, too.

Jace gazed off toward the parking lot as if he'd lost interest. Inside, he jitterbugged. Maneuvering the kid into an agreement was pretty sweet business.

"It's your call."

"Mr. Puckett says you work in wood and you're the best around."

He didn't know about that but he knew what Ned wanted to hear. "You can learn a lot from me. I plan to learn from you, too."

"Yeah?" He stood up a little straighter.

"The mask was genius."

"Yeah?" For the first time, the brown eye showed something besides hostility.

"I know rare talent when I see it." Every fiber of his being wanted to clap a hand on Ned's shoulder and show him some kindness, but with the chip residing on that shoulder like a weapon, Jace might get his head knocked off.

With the afternoon sun gleaming off his reddish hair and decision hanging on him like a coat, Ned looked to be exactly what he was. A troubled youth on the threshold of manhood, screaming for help and hope.

If someone had intervened with Jace at this age, he might have changed directions before it was too late.

Ned said, "I'm in."

"No skipping school."

"Ah, man. I hate school. School su—"

Jace cut off the common derogatory phrase before it could be uttered. "No skipping school. No drugs. No bad language. Shoot straight with me and I'll do the same. Character is more important than talent."

Ned tossed his hair to one side. The shaggy lock flopped back down. "You some kind of Jesus dude or something?"

Jesus dude.

"Yeah." Jace gave him a squint-eyed glare. "Is that a problem?"

Ned lifted both hands. "No. I'm cool with it. When do I start?"

First things first. "Do we have a deal?"

Ned looked at the offered hand and twitched a couple of times. "You're stuck on the school thing?"

"Nonnegotiable."

"I hate school."

Jace shrugged. The ball was in Ned's court and he was smart enough to know it.

Ned blew out a put-upon sigh, then lurched forward and shook hands. "Okay. Deal."

Jace stared at the new dose of trouble he'd just welcomed into his life and hoped he didn't live to regret it.

"Well, good morning. I haven't seen you around in a while."

Kitty had come out from cleaning one of the cabins to find Donny Babcock waiting for her. She'd glanced behind him, disappointed to see he was alone.

"Business in the city." He whipped a bouquet of flowers from behind his back. "Brought you these."

She shifted an armload of laundry to accept the pink daisies. "They're lovely. Thank you."

"Not as lovely as the recipient." His smile gleamed

bright and wide in the sunlight as he fell into step next to her.

"Well, thank you again." She stuck her nose in the flowers. "I haven't seen Jace in a few days, either. Did he go with you?"

It was a reasonable question. Maybe that's why Jace had sent someone else to do the repairs.

"Jace?" He smirked just a little. "No. I'm the business end of the deal. Jace does the labor."

Though he stopped short of degrading Jace, Kitty bristled. "Jace is a fine businessman."

He'd run his own contracting business long before Donny came into the picture.

"No insult intended." Donny pushed the laundry room door open for her. "Jace is the best. Absolutely the best. A man couldn't have a better friend."

The sound of construction work cut through the air. Donny's head turned toward the sound. "Is he here?"

Didn't the man hear a word she'd said?

"He sent someone in his place." She tried not to sound hurt over that turn of events.

"Too bad. I was going to lend a hand."

"Haven't you talked to him?" Kitty poked a load of whites into the tub, hoping Donny could give her some insight into Jace's sudden disappearance. She'd feel a lot better thinking Jace was away on business instead of believing he was avoiding her on purpose.

"Not much. We're both busy men. With our

schedules, we barely bump in the hallway. Jace has a new project going on in that shop he's so proud of. He stays out there all the time."

"I thought you worked with him."

"Not in the shop. The dust bothers me." He coughed slightly. "Allergies. But he's got help. Some kid's out there sawing and pounding half the night. They're building something for the Land Run celebration."

Kitty's hand paused on the washer controls. "Land Run? Really? I'm on that committee." She hadn't heard a thing about Jace building something. "What are they working on?"

Donny frowned. "I didn't pay that much attention. It looks like a merry-go-round to me."

"A merry-go-round?" Something fluttered in her memory. "Do you mean a carousel?"

"Yeah, that's what it is. Horses, brass rings and everything. He's got junk lying all over the place, parts of old ones, bits of new ones. The place is a beehive." Donny reached around her and pushed the starter knob. Water gushed from the jets into the metal tub. "I don't know why he's so interested in a bunch of old junk like that. But that's Jace. Living in the past and missing out." He reached for Kitty's hand and winked. "Old Donny boy, on the other hand, can see the beauty that's right in front of him. What's say you and me go get some lunch?"

Her heart banged hard against her rib cage but not because of Donny's invitation.

Jace was building a carousel?

✛ ✛ ✛

The long, metal workshop behind Jace's house was quiet at four o'clock in the morning. A few hours ago, before he'd succumbed to fatigue and grabbed a little sleep, the place had rocked with Ned's loud music coupled with the grind and buzz of power tools.

Jace crossed the threshold, shut the door behind him, and flipped on the lights. The workbenches and tables were littered with parts in progress, the scent of fresh wood and sawdust in the air. The carousel was coming along, with the addition of a couple of restorable chariots he'd found on the internet. They'd set him back more than he'd hoped, but even with them, he didn't see how they could have carousel ready in time. Thus, the short sleep and long hours.

He made his way to Ned's workstation. The teen had held up his end of the bargain so far and when he was in the shop, goggles in place and a piece of wood in hand, Ned was in the zone. Sometimes he forgot to eat. The kid was a true artist, lost in his creation.

As Jace rounded the table, his toe connected with something soft and he nearly stumbled.

"Ned?" Tonight wasn't the first time he'd come in to find his employee asleep on a drop cloth, his head cradled by a tattered black jacket. Didn't anybody worry about this kid other than Jace?

Ned stirred and sat up. His hair was a rusty nest against the side of his head. "What time is it?"

"Too early. Go home and get some sleep."

"I'm good." He unwound his thin body and stood, arching his back in a stretch.

"How late did you work after I went to bed?"

Ned twitched. "Don't know." He went to the workbench and lifted a carved horse face. Fatigue bagged his eyes and drooped his shoulders. "What do you think?"

"I think it's great. I also think there's a reason you're not going home at night."

Ned's expression flattened. "So?"

For once, Jace hated being right. "So go in the house. My air mattress is still up. Get some sleep. I'll wake you for school in a few hours."

Ned hesitated for less than a blink before staggering out of the workshop.

Jace picked up a sander and flipped the switch, thinking as he worked. He shouldn't get involved in the kid's home life. Didn't want to get involved. But he knew he was going to.

"You bunking over again tonight?" Jace shot the sandpaper sharply over the weathered mane of a stander, a carousel horse with his legs on the ground.

It was Saturday, the one full day Jace gave to the project. For the last three days, Ned had slept on the floor in Jace's living room. On the second day, Jace had bought another air mattress. Since then Ned had slept like the dead. His attitude had improved, too, and as far as Jace could tell, he didn't go anywhere but here and school. As long as he was one place or the other, he wasn't getting into trouble.

"If you're cool with it." The kid hated going home and no one ever came looking. Once, Jace had offered to call his parents but Ned had walked out and not returned until the next afternoon.

"Anytime." Jace shot him a grin. "When you're on-site, I can get more work out of you."

Ned snorted and went back to replacing a leg joint.

For a normally solitary guy, Jace was still a little surprised to find himself with two houseguests.

"We're never going to finish in time."

Jace arched an eyebrow. "You quitting on me?"

Ned bristled, his brown eye shooting daggers. "Just saying."

Considering that he was over his head on this project already, Jace was just as worried as Ned, but he wasn't ready to give up. How did he squeeze a four-month project into a matter of weeks? "I can't do this without you."

A slow, rare grin lifted Ned's cheeks. "I figured that out. That's why you gave me a raise."

Jace chuckled. His new employee was testy and brooding, but Jace liked him. Ned was shockingly reliable, completely devoted to the art and other than one day of skipped school that he refused to explain, he'd kept his end of the bargain. More than that, there was a vulnerability about the kid that got to Jace.

"I know a couple of other guys in shop that might help out. They could do the grunt work." He gave a sly grin. "They might even do it pro bono for a chance to work with you."

"What are you talking about?"

Ned hiked one shoulder. "We need help. You got a good rep. A couple guys I know wouldn't mind learning from you."

Jace carefully laid the tool aside and stared at the mess around him. He'd never considered taking on more help. He was a solitary man, unused to letting people in. If he got too close he'd be in trouble. But this town had taken him in, given him a successful life. He wanted to give them the carousel. More than that, he wanted to do it for Kitty.

Most of the horses only needed to be sanded down and repainted, but the detail had to be exact. That required a skilled artist like Ned or a man with experience such as himself. Still, the sanding, stripping and even reassembling could be taught pretty easily.

"Let me think about it."

The shop door scraped open, metal against concrete, and Jace looked up, expecting Donny. Since the last excursion when he'd returned with a pocketful of money, Donny had been in a fine mood. Jace was still wondering about that.

It wasn't Donny Babcock who came strolling into the shop.

Jace's heart lurched and his mouth went dry. "Kitty."

He'd been so careful to stay away, to let someone else do the repairs on her motel. What was she doing here?

Chapter Twelve

Kitty stopped inside the door and glanced around the ordered clutter that was Jace's workshop. He hadn't brought her here the day of the picnic but she'd seen the large metal building.

"Am I interrupting something?" She twisted the clasp on her clutch purse.

From the sudden silence in the workshop and the curious looks of both Jace and his red-haired helper, she figured the answer was yes.

She squared her shoulders. Be brave, Kitty.

If Jace didn't want her here, she'd know soon enough.

Jace put aside some sort of power tool and came toward her. "Come on in."

His voice held a question. What was she doing here? She was asking herself the same question, even though she knew the answers. Both Cheyenne and GI Jack had Kitty seriously thinking about her feelings for Jace. There was something there worth pursuing.

Though she worried about her in-laws' response, she'd spent a lot of time in prayer, too. No answer had fallen from heaven but she hadn't felt condemned, either. Donny's announcement about the carousel had tipped the scales. She wanted to see Jace and she wanted to know about the project.

"I don't want to bother you."

"You're fine."

Not very reassuring, but not an outright rejection, either.

"I see you took my advice and hired an assistant."

Jace's eyes brightened—just a bit but enough that Kitty felt less of an interloper. He gestured toward the redhead who'd pushed his goggles on top of his head and stood staring at her with an annoyed expression.

"This is my right-hand man, Ned Veech."

A smile bloomed inside Kitty. He'd hired Ned. What a sweet thing to do. "Ned, hello. I remember you from Sunday school. You might have grown a little since then."

Ned's insolent stare evaporated. "I guess I have. How ya doin', Ms. Wainright? I didn't recognize you for a minute. You a friend of Jace's?"

Kitty held her smile in place but her gaze skittered to Jace's face. "We attend the same church."

"Oh, yeah. That's cool." His red hair was too long and flopped forward when he nodded. The boy Kitty remembered was still in there somewhere, but time had taken a toll. Ned was grubby-looking as always, but instead of the childish innocence she recalled, there was a wary hardness around him.

"You're always welcome to come back." She kept the invitation light and escapable.

"Thanks." He flipped the goggles back in place. "I gotta get to work."

That went over well.

"Was there something you needed, Kitty?" Jace had shoved both palms in his hip pockets.

"I'm bothering you. I should go." She started to turn. A strong hand caught her elbow.

"No." When she looked over her shoulder, he dropped her arm. His voice softened. "You're not bothering anyone."

"Really? You're sure?"

"Positive." His smile was real. "Would you like a tour of a mad carpenter's workshop?"

She laughed, as much from relief as pleasure. "I'd love one."

"I guess you can tell what we're working on." He lifted a painted horse's head.

Kitty's pulse jumped. "So the rumor is true. Oh, Jace. Why didn't you tell me? Where did you find it? Who had it?" She pressed her palms to her cheeks. "Oh, I'm talking too much, but the committee will be thrilled to bits. I know I certainly am. Why didn't you call me?"

Okay, she'd asked the crucial question but in a way that Jace would never suspect how bewildered and yes, hurt, she'd been when he'd gone silent after their lovely picnic.

Was that just a tad of excitement she spotted in those quiet eyes? "I wanted it to be a surprise."

He'd wanted to surprise her? He'd done this for her? Her pulse skittered, stopped and started again.

"Redemption's been good to me. Giving something back was the least I could do."

The thrill fizzled. He hadn't done this for her. He'd done it for the town.

Which was just as well, better even.

She was so confused.

Cheyenne's words kept running through her head. The trinket box scripture wasn't far behind. Her friends were putting crazy thoughts in her head. If she wasn't careful, they'd cause her to embarrass herself and hurt Trina and Chuck. Her in-laws would be appalled to know her reasons for being here. Worse, they'd be devastated that dating again had even crossed her mind.

And yet it had.

She bit the inside of her cheek, trying hard to think of anything except how good Jace looked with wood chips in his hair, covered in sawdust and surrounded by the tools of his trade. His skin had darkened, begun to bronze since she'd last seen him. The effect gilded his hair and changed his eyes to a soft green. He must be working outside somewhere.

A beautifully painted horse body stood on a

sawhorse behind Jace. She went to it, as much for something to do, as to see the incredible work.

"Is this from the original carousel?"

"It is. You were right about asking Popbottle Jones."

"He knew?" When Jace nodded, she said, "Maybe this is the same one Opal Banks rode after that awful gypsy kissed her."

Jace's eyes crinkled in humor. "Maybe."

"Wouldn't that be amazing? Just think of the history we're looking at, Jace. Think of the people who've ridden this pony, of the laughing children, the romantic couples, the silly, giddy girls like Opal. This pony could tell so many stories."

"I like thinking about them, too."

Kitty stroked light fingers over the glossy paint. "Where did you find it? I still can't believe you did. I was afraid it was lost forever."

"Most of the main body and the horses were in storage in a shed at Simmy John's place."

"Why would Simmy John have it?"

"When the carousel was dismantled, his daddy bought it from the city on a sentimental whim." Jace dusted an imaginary speck from the horse's mane. "Simmy John's daddy proposed to his mother on horse number six. So when the town dismantled the carousel during the war, he bought what was left, stored it away, and it was eventually forgotten."

"What a sweet story."

"Yes, and Simmy John was happy to hear it might

be used again. We were both amazed at the condition. Even the music apparatus still plays. We have to rebuild the base and the metal portions, and a couple of the horse heads needed complete renovation. That's where Ned comes in." He ran a hand along the smooth, glossy paint of one of the finished prancers. She was a beauty with the saddle work done in bright aqua, red and yellow. "He did most of this one."

Ned had paused in his buzzing and scraping to watch the other two admire his handiwork. He might want to appear cool, but his one uncovered eye begged for approval.

Poor boy. What had he been through since she'd taught him about Jesus?

"Ned, you are incredibly gifted. Thank you for sharing your talent with the rest of us."

One shoulder jerked. He cranked some kind of grinding tool and drowned out further compliments.

Kitty lifted an eyebrow at Jacc. "Did I say something wrong? Is he okay?"

"He's a little touchy. Mostly, he doesn't know how to take a compliment."

Kitty turned her body so Ned wouldn't know he was the topic of discussion. "Has he told you anything about his family?"

"No, but he doesn't go home anymore. He's bunking here."

"There's no home to go to, from what I understand."

"No family? I thought he has a mother."

Kitty shook her head. "She's in and out. Mostly out. Last I heard she'd moved to Muskogee with a new boyfriend. That's been at least a year ago. He had a brother, Jerry, the man who drowned in Redemption River a few weeks ago. The one you tried to save."

Jace's mouth fell open. "You're kidding. Jerry was Ned's brother?"

"A half brother, I think. Their names were different, but he was all the family Ned had."

"Why didn't I know that?"

She shrugged. "I suppose everyone took for granted you did."

"Unbelievable. No other relatives?"

"I don't think so. When Ned was small, his father was in the picture but he's not anymore. As far as I know, Ned is all alone."

Eyes squinted in thought, Jace slowly pivoted toward his employee. "A lot of things make sense now."

At seventeen, Ned was still underage. How had he avoided social services?

Kitty followed his gaze. "You're doing a good thing, Jace. He needs you."

The thought made him uncomfortable, all things considered. He hadn't hired Ned out of concern for the boy. He'd hired him selfishly because he'd wanted to please Kitty. "He's an employee."

"Who sleeps in your house."

"On my floor."

"Just as you do."

Jace couldn't stop the quick bark of laughter. "Don't make a hero out of me."

"If the shoe fits…" Twirling a curl with an index finger, she widened her eyes and arched her shoulders.

His heart had done all kinds of gymnastics the minute she'd walked through the door. The rational part of his brain had demanded he send her away but the rest of him was glad to see her. Redemption was a small town. He couldn't avoid her forever.

And okay, he didn't want to. He'd been close to her nearly every day for several years now and not seeing her was like cutting off an arm.

Today her pale, pale hair was wadded into a knot at the back of her head. Loose, thick strands curved around her face and brushed her shoulders. A couple of combs poked out from beneath an overhang of blondness. He'd never seen a woman whose hair could look pretty and messy at the same time.

He hadn't thought it possible, but Kitty had gotten prettier since the day she'd picnicked in his yard and he'd nearly kissed her.

Sometimes he regretted not following through, but the result would have been disaster. No matter how many excuses he created to make kissing her all right, it wouldn't have been.

No matter what Popbottle Jones had said, she was

out of his league, and he was out of his mind for even thinking such a thing was possible.

God, he loved her so much. She'd swirled into his shop like a warm spring breeze ripe with fragrance and smiles and now that she was here, he wanted to keep her. Forever.

He picked up a slab of planed hardwood, smoothed a hand down it. This piece was ready to glue. "Don't get your hopes up about the carousel."

"What do you mean?"

"I doubt we'll finish in time for the celebration. Ned's a genius but I have to study as I go. Restoring carousels is not my area."

"These you've done are beautiful, Jace. Incredible, really."

"The horses might be ready by then, but what about the base and the pavilion top? Neither requires too much expertise, only basic carpentry skills, but they take time." He shook his head, mouth rueful. "I don't know what I was thinking."

She touched his arm and he felt her warmth all the way to his heart. "You were thinking of the pleasure this would bring to others."

No, he'd been thinking of himself. And her.

"When I tell the committee about this, they're going to want it. Couldn't you hire some more help?"

"I can't spare the money." He'd pushed his Queen Anne to the background because of the carousel. Eventually, he'd need money to finish her.

"The committee has some funds to spend."

"Seriously?"

"I can help, too. In fact, I want to. This was my idea to begin with. Why should you be stuck with all the work?"

"I don't know."

Kitty wiggled her fingers in his face. "These fingers can paint. I'm terrific with detail."

"You are?"

"Who do you think paints all those figurines? And the bobblehead dolls?"

"You?"

"Little old me." She laughed and spun in a semicircle taking in the contents of the workshop. "We can do this, Jace. There are others who will help, too, for a chance at bringing the carousel to life again. We may not be experts, but we can follow directions from an expert."

He was starting to catch her enthusiasm. "When can you start?"

She clasped her hands in front of her. "Give me a paintbrush and point me in the right direction."

Kitty was a whirlwind organizer when she set her mind to something. And this carousel stirred something deep inside her. Spending every day in Jace's workshop wasn't a bad idea either. She figured she could explore and analyze the feelings simmering between them. She'd stopped wondering if Jace liked her. He had a natural reserve, an aloofness she found intriguing, but when she said his name, he dropped what he was doing and came her way. Just as he'd been doing for years, though she'd never noticed.

She was noticing now.

He was across the room with Ned and a couple of other men. Her gaze found him often throughout the day, as it did now. He always seemed to know because he looked up and grinned every time.

She grinned back, wrinkled her nose and waved a paintbrush, wishing she knew how to run a table saw so she could work on that side of the room.

The workshop was huge and with the addition of volunteers, Jace had arranged the room into sections. Power tools and woodworking on one side. Paint and assembly on the other. Refurbishing the music box and the metal works in still another. The clang and clatter, buzz and grind were a backdrop to conversations and the come and go of volunteers.

"Things are shaping up."

GI Jack, with paint in his hair and wood chips stuck to his shirt, stood next to her at the assembly-line style table. He and Popbottle Jones had embraced the project with enthusiasm. All her friends were here when they weren't working, Annie and Cheyenne, Sloan and Trace, Jilly and Jeri from the vet clinic, the pastor and another dozen guys and girls from church and the Land Run Committee.

Jace had been particular about who took part, carefully putting the right people in the right places. Other than a few mistakes here and there, the volunteers were doing well.

"Another week and we'll be ready to move everything to the town square."

"I figure Ida June and Sunny will have the pavilion ready by then, too." He cackled softly. "You should stop by and watch those two at work. What a pair."

Kitty laughed with him. She and Sunny Case were nearly the same age and Ida June Click was in her eighties. Though different as night and day, both wielded a mighty hammer and loved a project. Together with most of the shop class from the high school, they'd partnered up to build the pavilion on which the carousel would rest. Those kids would learn more from Ida June's badgering and pithy quotations than they'd thought possible.

"I love the way the town has come together behind this project."

The lumberyard donated most of the wood. Simmy John Case's hardware store provided tools and paint. The Land Run Committee, the banks and the Markovas had chipped in funds for the metalwork being done by an out-of-town contractor.

"Right inspiring, ain't it?"

Kitty dabbed red paint onto a horse's breast harness. "Very." And she was thrilled to be part of it.

"I could use a sody pop. How about you?"

She shook her head, smiling. "I'm good. Thank you though."

"How about the rest of you?" GI sent the message down the line, receiving yesses from a pair of men assembling the legs onto a standing pony.

He carefully tilted his paintbrush into a jar of solvent and rubbed his palms down the sides of his pants, leaving streaks of green and pink. "Back in a bit."

He shuffled off, leaving Kitty with a smile and a warm feeling as she returned to carefully adding tiny crimson beads across the front of the horse.

"Who's minding the motel office today?"

Kitty jumped at the sudden masculine voice next to her ear. Donny Babcock had a way of sneaking up and invading her space. She ducked slightly to the side, dismayed to see a streak of unexpected red on the white-bodied horse. She reached quickly for a rag dampened with paint thinner.

"You startled me."

Dressed in jeans and a T-shirt instead of his usual business suit, Donny looked different, but like so many others, he was doing his part to make the carousel a reality. She couldn't fault him there, although she did wonder about the allergies he'd claimed to have.

"I saw you standing here all alone and thought you could use some company." He put his hand over hers, stilling the work on the horse. With a proprietary air, he took the pungent-odored cloth from her fingers and wiped away the unwanted paint.

Kitty hid a sigh. She wasn't alone. The room was packed. He was probably being gallant but just the same, she pulled her hand away.

"Harvey's on duty at the office." Harvey was one of

her full-time boarders, a retired widower. His grandson was president of the bank but Harvey preferred living independently in the motel to living in his son's fancy house. "He's having a domino tournament on the front lawn."

"Sounds fun." Donny smiled his toothy smile. "There. I think I've taken care of your little mess-up. Want to take some time off, go inside and grab a bite to eat? Relax those weary fingers? Our refrigerator's full."

The refrigerator was Jace's but she didn't say that. Donny had a way of wording things that irritated her and she needed to get over it.

"The church ladies went on full alert when they discovered Jace's cupboards were bare."

"A blessing to us all. So what do you say? Let's go in and have some of that fried chicken and talk awhile."

"I want to finish this first, Donny. You go ahead."

He seemed genuinely perplexed at her refusal. "Are you sure?"

"Positive." She added a smile to the refusal.

"All right then. Maybe later. Have you thought about our last conversation?"

Kitty focused on the next bead, hand steady, but mind busy. She'd been considering Donny's offer for a while. He wanted her to invest in his real estate business, with the promise of making a lot of money. "I haven't decided yet."

"You don't want to miss out on this, Kitty. Prices go up every day. Did your mother-in-law tell you about the return on her investment?"

"She's really excited about it." Trina and Chuck had invested with Donny and had already made several thousand dollars. Kitty had to admit she was impressed. "They've been telling me I should invest."

"You should."

"I'm praying about it."

Something flickered across Donny's face but his smile was the usual. "Don't wait too long or you'll miss out on the chance of a lifetime."

The buzz and hum of activity heavy around him, Jace swallowed back the knot in his throat. He was overwhelmed. Grateful. Terrified. Sometimes he woke up in the night sweating with anxiety. All these people underfoot and in his house and shop all day and half the night. He loved it. He hated it. Though he'd been a part of Redemption for a long time, he'd remained on the perimeter, an outsider looking in. He'd never really fit. Never belonged. He'd simply lived and worked here. Now, he was right in the middle of the activity and it scared him spitless.

He threaded a screw onto a screwdriver, glad for the familiar feel of work in his hands. The best thing about the community involvement was Kitty. He looked up, saw her talking to Donny and sighed. Was it his imagination or did every single man in the room manage to find an excuse to stop and talk to her?

There were other beautiful women in the room, some of them single. Why did Kitty stand out like a bright yellow butterfly?

He drilled the screw into place, tossed the tool to the tabletop, and crossed the room. Ned looked up, saw his direction and smirked. Jace pointed a finger at him. Ned's smirk widened. Smart aleck kid could read his mind.

Donny had become a regular in the workshop since the project began. He'd shouldered his share of the work. More than that, Jace had noticed how the other volunteers related to him. They clapped him on the shoulder, laughed with him and seemed to genuinely like the guy. Apparently Jace was the one with the problem, not Donny.

That much, at least, was a relief.

Seeing Donny cozy up to Kitty wasn't.

Donny said something close to her ear, smiled and touched her hair before ambling toward the door.

Jealousy tightened Jace's gut into knots and set his mind racing. No matter how clean Donny might be now, he hadn't always been. Kitty deserved better. The way Jace saw it, if she was coming out of her widow's cocoon he should run interference and protect her from the wolves until the right guy came along.

"Hey," he said. "Ready for a break? I'm buying."

She laughed, knowing as he did that the kitchen

was full of donated food and drink. "Big spender. So generous of you, but I just turned Donny down."

"Why does that make me happy?"

"I don't know. Why does it?" She dabbed a coat of dazzling turquoise onto a wooden eye.

Jace didn't figure he should answer that. "He's not good enough for you."

"Oh." She seemed disappointed by his answer.

"Let's walk outside, get some air."

"I'd like that."

Chapter Thirteen

The shop was mercifully silent as Jace cleaned up his tools for the night. He'd sent Ned to bed thirty minutes ago, convincing the workaholic teen that he needed to sleep before school. Beside Jace, Kitty sealed paint cans and gathered brushes for cleaning.

She'd stayed, as she had every night, until the rest of the volunteers drifted home to rest and only the pair of them remained in the shop. Even though his body ached with fatigue from long days and late nights, he looked forward to this time. Kitty had to be exhausted, too, but she never seemed to fade.

"We're almost there," he said, breaking what had been a companionable quiet for the past fifteen minutes.

"Another week, you think?" she asked. Her hair had come undone in several places and hung in strands down her neck and around her face. She hooked one troublesome lock over an ear.

"Maybe sooner. Sunny texted me. The pavilion is

ready when we are. Other than Ned's special project, which he won't let anyone see, we should start assembling the remaining pieces by Wednesday, test the music and mechanics, do a little touch-up and we're there."

"And you didn't think we could finish in time," she teased.

His grin rested on her pixie face. "You have paint on your nose."

"You have paint speckles…everywhere."

"Spraying does that for you, especially when the guy next to you gets a little crazy with his." From the work sink, he dampened a cloth with water and soap. "Come here."

He tilted her chin with one hand and scrubbed gently at the side of her nose. Unable to resist the excuse to touch her, he turned her small face this way and that, wiping away speckles and imaginary spots. Her skin was velvet beneath his sandpaper fingers.

She held very still and smiled the entire time, blue eyes watching him. "That tickles."

"All done." But he didn't loosen his hold. "You're perfect again."

Her smile widened. "Good to know."

Jace dropped his hand but not his gaze. When had he become so comfortable with her that they could be alone this way without anxiety?

"Hungry?"

She shook her head. "I wouldn't mind some hot tea."

He frowned. "Do I have any?"

Kitty's laugh was short and sweet. "You've been invaded by women. You'll be amazed at the things you find in that kitchen."

"I already am. My refrigerator had an asthma attack last night. Who knew an appliance could have food allergies?"

His joke was met by a giggle that sent chill bumps up his spine. He could listen to that giggle all night.

"Did it wheeze?"

"Something awful."

"Oh, poor thing. Shall we go inside and make sure it's okay?"

Jace flipped off all the light switches except the entry, locked down the bay doors, and double-checked that everything was secure before leading the way to the Queen Anne. She stood tall and elegant, if lonely-looking, beneath the gray-blue light of a crescent moon.

"What's that star?" She paused to point upward. A bright point of light rested in the cradle of the moon.

"Mars maybe?" he asked, trying to remember the high school science he'd mostly slept through.

"Is Mars a star?"

"You're asking a man who barely passed high school." He couldn't believe he'd admitted that.

"That's not true. You're too smart and too good at what you do to have slacked in school."

"Everything I know was learned through the school of hard work."

"Where did you go to school, Jace?"

He hesitated, not wanting to get into his past, but aware that not answering would bring suspicion. "Oklahoma City. You've lived here all your life, haven't you?"

"Since birth. Mother and Dad were both natives, too, which made it really strange when they moved to Africa after I married Dave. They'd always talked about Africa and wanted to be missionaries but I couldn't believe they'd do it."

By now, they'd reached the back porch, a four-step rise to the door. The hinges groaned when Jace pushed it open.

"Creepy." Kitty gave a mock shudder.

"If you want creepy, try the turret this time of night." He reached around her narrow shoulders to flip on the inside light.

"I'd think the view of the sky is gorgeous from up there." She tilted her face toward him. In the buttery light, her eyes gleamed. "But creepy."

Jace considered inviting her up to see for herself, but thought better of the idea. Last time had been near disaster. Though he was handling her presence better now, no use taking a chance.

Flipping on lights as they went, he led the way into the kitchen. "No table. Sorry."

"The bar is fine. Got any folding chairs?"

Jace pulled a couple of metal chairs from a broom closet. "My fine dining furniture," he said.

Kitty was already rummaging in the pantry.

"Did you know you have graham crackers and marshmallows?"

"You'll probably find chocolate, too. Ned likes s'mores." When she glanced around, a question in her expression, he said, "Me, too."

"Oh, good. Nothing like s'mores and raspberry tea after a hard day at the carousel factory." The pilot igniter clicked and metal clanked as she set the tea-kettle to heat.

He loathed hot tea. "I'll have milk. We do have milk, don't we?"

With all the volunteers in and out of his house each day, he never knew what he'd find in the kitchen. While Kitty made s'mores, he poured the milk, then handed her a mug emblazoned with the logo of a building supplier and a couple of golden carnival glass saucers.

"Eclectic taste," he said when she raised an amused eyebrow at the antique dishes.

Her quick, ready smile flashed. "I like a man with discerning taste. Here, discern this." She aimed a s'more at his mouth. "Tell me if there's too much chocolate."

He bit obediently. Cracker crunched, chocolate gushed out the sides, and strings of hot marshmallow stretched from her fingers to his lips. He wanted to laugh but couldn't.

Giggling, she let him take control.

He devoured the small snack in one more bite. "Perfect."

She put the saucer of s'mores on the bar and handed him a paper towel. "Now you know the depth of my culinary expertise."

"Any woman who can make s'mores has my heart."

She took the comment as the intended joke, waving him to the bar. "Oh, sit down and drink your milk before you choke."

They settled across from each other, Kitty's fragrant tea sending up smoke signals in the center.

"The carousel has interfered with your work on the house, hasn't it?" she asked.

"She's an ongoing project." He sipped his milk. "Could take years."

"Still, you're generous to give up your time, your shop."

"My peace and quiet."

"That's the worst of it, isn't it? You're a very private person, and now all this."

"Gotta love the shower of groceries. Ned and Donny thought I was a miser for not stocking up."

"They know where the grocery store is."

"Yeah, I guess they do. But they're guests."

"How are things going with Ned?"

"Okay." He broke the corner of his second s'more but didn't eat. "I talked to Jessie Rainmaker."

"About his lack of family?"

Jace nodded. "He said if social services wanted to get involved at this late hour, I could always apply for guardianship until Ned turns eighteen."

"You'd do that?"

The prospect scared him mindless. "He already lives here for the most part. I can't dump him on the street. Or wherever he was living."

Her expression softened. "Jace, that's incredibly generous. You are such a good man."

"I wouldn't go that far. Remember, I'm working the kid into exhaustion."

"He loves every minute of it. Do you know I even heard him laugh today? I didn't know he could."

"He's coming along. I think he's scared to death most of the time."

"Of what?"

Jace shrugged. "Life. Himself. The future. I don't know."

But he did know, of course. He'd been in Ned's shoes, only he'd had a mother who'd loved him and begged him not to run with the gangs. He'd taken his first joyride in a stolen Subaru when he was fourteen. Though he'd gotten a slap on the wrist from the law, his mother had cried for days. His stint in Lexington had killed her.

"He needs Jesus."

"Agreed. He's prickly, though. I'm going easy."

"He watches everything you do."

The knowledge and responsibility of that truth hung on him like an iron anchor. What if he made a misstep? It wouldn't be the first time, and he already had enough on his conscience.

"Lousy about his brother."

"Have you mentioned Jerry to him?"

"We talked. He's pretty torn up, as you can imagine. He was supposed to go fishing with Jerry that day but backed out for some reason. He thinks if he'd been there…"

"Poor Ned. He couldn't have changed the outcome. He might have even drowned trying to help his brother." She rose, taking her teacup. "You know, in a way, he kind of reminds me of Donny."

Jace nearly choked on his milk. "How's that?"

"Needy, but not wanting anyone to know."

Jace frowned. "Donny?"

"In a different way than Ned but still very needy for acceptance. I think he brags a little too much and is pushy and arrogant because he's longing for approval. Sometimes I feel sorry for him."

Jace had considered Donny a user and a loser, not as needy. Leave it to someone with a pure heart to see something else.

"You're a very nice woman." And he was a poor excuse for a Christian. Unlike his own mentor, he'd done nothing but expect the worst. He'd never encouraged. He'd discouraged. He'd done his share of complaining, too.

Lord forgive him.

"Want another s'more?" Eyebrows raised, she hefted the marshmallow package.

"I wouldn't turn it down." He followed her to the counter where he poked two marshmallows on the end of a fork and stuck them into a burner flame. The marshmallows caught fire and blackened, earning an "Eww," from Kitty who was busy melting chocolate chips in the microwave.

"This is the fine cuisine of a bachelor." He peeled the black crust off the bottom one and popped the sticky lump into his mouth, then waved the fork under her nose. "Try it."

She clamped her mouth tight and shook her head, holding up a graham cracker as a shield. He wiggled the burnt mess closer. Kitty made a noise and took a step back, eyes twinkling above her cracker shield.

He would later wonder what had come over him, but Jace leaned in and snapped the cracker with his teeth. As soon as he did, the flimsy shield between them disappeared and they were mere inches apart. So close in fact that he could see the tiny pulse beat in her throat and feel the soft puff of her breath against his hand.

He swallowed. The dry cracker stuck in his throat. But he paid it no mind. All he could see was Kitty. All he could think was how happy he'd felt in the time they'd been working together. She was a pearl of great price. A rare gift.

He braced one hand against the wall next to her head. The sticky fork slapped against his pristinely painted wall. With the other hand, he touched her face and when she smiled, he leaned in, heart hammering in his chest.

His head said no. His heart said yes.

"You have chocolate right there." He touched the corner of her mouth.

Her eyes brightened. "Can you get that for me?"

Jace's heart stopped beating, then started again in a wild rat-a-tat-tat.

"My pleasure."

Cherished. Kitty felt cherished.

She'd never fully understood the term before, but now, when Jace held her face in his workman's fingers and kissed her with exquisite tenderness, she knew.

She gave herself up to the beauty and sweetness of the moment. Jace tasted of marshmallows and graham crackers with the hint of chocolate mixed in. Or perhaps that was her. Her lips curved beneath his and he answered with a smile of his own as he slowly, gently, regrettably pulled away.

He stayed close, holding her lightly, and she was glad. Her bones had turned to jelly and she thought she might slide down the wall like a swooning heroine in a silent movie.

"I haven't kissed anyone in a long time," she admitted.

The last man she'd kissed had been Dave at the airport before he'd left for Afghanistan. She thought she should feel guilty, but she didn't.

She wondered what that meant.

"Me, either. Not in a very long time."

She loved his voice, tender and strong all at once. "How was it?"

Those talented lips curved again. "I think I need more practice."

Kitty laughed and tilted her face upward. "Me, too."

Chuckle rumbling in his chest, he moved in to place his smile against hers. It was a joyous meeting and Kitty wanted to laugh and sing all at once.

She'd never expected to come to this point in her life where she'd even consider letting another man hold and kiss her.

But the reality was wonderful.

Jace Carter was the special man her heart must have been waiting for.

Spirit soaring and happy, she slid her arms around Jace's strong back, laid her head on his shoulder and held him close.

The fork he held clattered to the floor as he embraced her. The rugged hands that could build a house wielded such tender power.

Voice muffled against him, Kitty admitted, "I never thought I'd do this again. I never thought I'd want to."

His hand stroked the back of her hair. His voice was husky. "Me, either."

She wondered again if he'd been married and burned by the experience.

"Who hurt you, Jace?"

His body stiffened, and his breathing accelerated as though she'd hit a nerve. He held her tighter, his voice muffled against her hair.

"Mostly myself." The cryptic answer told her nothing. "This isn't about me. It's you, Kitty. Are you going to be okay with this?"

"I don't know." It wasn't as if she'd planned to kiss him. It wasn't as if she'd set out to have feelings for him. What these feelings were, she wasn't sure yet, but they were strong enough to tempt her from her widowhood. "But I want to find out."

He gently pulled back until only their hands were touching. From his expression, he was suffering the same confusion and happiness she felt.

These were uncharted waters for both of them.

His eyes were gentle on her face, his lips curved. "What was in those s'mores?"

She lifted an eyebrow, teasing. "I don't know. Want another one?"

Jace started kicking himself as soon as he'd walked Kitty to her car and said good-night. He'd done a major piece of stupid. Major. Made worse because Kitty had kissed him back.

Leaning on the bar, he dropped his head and closed his eyes. He'd let himself forget everything except how sweet and beautiful and amazing Kitty felt in his arms. No one had held him close in years and when she'd touched him, he'd been lost. Kitty's sweetness, her tenderness, her pure Christian love, had filled a dark hole inside him. Would she want to touch him if she knew?

Not likely.

He groaned, confused and thrilled all at once and completely terrified.

What had he started? What was he going to do about it?

He didn't know.

Love was a good and beautiful thing. But he wasn't.

With a troubled shove, he set about to straighten the kitchen.

For years, he'd had no difficulty keeping a distance from people, particularly women, but Kitty wrecked havoc on his self-control.

Dishes clattered into the dishwasher. He dumped lemon-scented soap into the dispenser.

How did he protect the woman he loved from unsuitable men when he was one of them? Life had been easier when she'd been adamantly a widow.

Yet, in the past few weeks, since the carousel project began, he'd come to realize she wasn't as adamant as before.

Then tonight—his heart quivered—tonight she'd stepped over his once unbreachable wall and charged inside.

Did a man like him dare hope?

The back door groaned and Jace pivoted, dish detergent box in hand.

"Que pasa, amigo?" Donny said.

The penchant for random Spanish phrases was annoying but, like his tendency to exaggerate, harmless. He entered the kitchen with a breezy stride. At some point, he'd changed from casual work to business attire. After Kitty's comments, Jace wondered if Donny's fondness for fancy suits fueled a flagging self-concept.

Why hadn't he seen, as Kitty had, the wounds in his former cellmate? He knew better than she the desperate details of Donny's misspent youth. Yet he'd ignored the signs, more interested in protecting himself than in helping the man who'd alerted the prison guards to save Jace's life. A man shouldn't forget something like that.

"You're out late."

"Visiting with Pastor Parker and his family. Nice people."

Donny took orange juice from the fridge, poured a glass and swallowed it down. Then he added the empty glass to the opened dishwasher. Had he been doing those things all along and Jace hadn't bothered to notice?

"Need some help in here?"

"I've got it." Jace put away the marshmallows and graham crackers, trying not to think of their sweet taste on Kitty's lips. "Everything all right with you?"

"Couldn't be much better. Life is, as they say—" he kissed the tips of his fingers "—sweet."

"Got a minute? I have something that needs saying."

"So speak." Donny braced both hands on the bar behind him and slouched, expression tense. He must be expecting another blast of warnings. Jace had been forthcoming with those.

"You've been good help on the carousel project. Thanks."

Donny straightened, his swagger back. "No problem, bro. The people are great. The project worthy. 'Donny,' I said to myself, 'old Jacey boy needs your help.' So here I am."

"I've noticed. I appreciate your effort. What I'm trying to say is this. I'm a Christian. Or claim to be. But I haven't acted like one. Not with you."

"Hey, forget it. So, you got a little scared when I showed up after all this time. You got a lot to lose, pal. A lot. This town thinks you walk on water."

"I wouldn't go that far, but they respect me. I worked hard to earn a good reputation, and I've been afraid of losing it." Jace folded a tea towel in quarters. He wasn't wild about spilling his guts, especially to Donny, but he owed him this.

"Figured as much. Men like us have to work harder than others to prove our worth." Donny's display of teeth fell short of being a smile. "Especially to ourselves."

He was right. And this was the first purely honest thing Donny had shared with him.

"We talked about second chances when you first came, but I haven't cut you any slack. You're trying, maybe you've really changed. As a Christian I owe the benefit of the doubt to everyone. I want you to know something. I'm going to be a better friend. If you need to talk, pray, whatever. I'm here."

"Thanks, bro. You're a pal. Always knew I could count on you." Donny shoved off the counter to clap him on the shoulder. "I have some computer work to finish before I can earn my beauty rest. Sleep tight."

The kitchen grew silent after Donny left. Milo padded in, stretched and yawned, looking up at Jace with curious brown eyes. Jace rubbed his soft ears.

"Did I wake you?"

The pup was irresistible. He sat on his bottom, one leg cocked at the same angle as his head, adoration in the soft brown eyes. If the rest of the world thought as much of him as Milo, he'd be king of the universe. "Give me another minute, okay?"

He didn't feel silly talking to Milo. Until the invasion of people, he and the little dog had had lots of one-sided conversations.

With the pup waiting patiently, Jace folded the metal chairs and stored them away. The talk with Donny hadn't been as satisfying as he'd hoped but he'd said the words. Now he had to get his actions and heart into line.

Which brought him full circle to the other heart problem.

What was he going to do about Kitty?

Chapter Fourteen

"This is so exciting."

Kitty hopped up and down and clapped her hands with such enthusiasm Jace laughed. He was a glutton for punishment, but he'd wanted to be with her when the carousel went up. Her reaction was every bit as good as he'd expected.

The official carousel opening wouldn't happen until the Land Run celebration, but today they were setting everything in place and testing the mechanics.

Jace was on the circular wooden platform helping Ned thread a brightly painted pony onto the metal pole that would provide its movement. The prancer was the first of two dozen restored animals to go up, along with three chariots.

A local trucking firm had moved the horses and body of the carousel to the city park, and a dozen city workers helped position the ride beneath the newly built pavilion.

A smattering of Jace's volunteers was there, too,

eager to see the fulfillment of long hours and late nights. Along with Nate and his friends from the shop class, they unloaded carefully wrapped ponies from a truck bed and carried them inside the covered pavilion. Kitty, Cheyenne, Ida June and Sunny Case had stopped screwing miniature bulbs into the unending number of light sockets to watch the first pony mounted.

A reporter from the *Redemption Register* appeared, snapping photos. He spotted the exuberant Kitty and pointed the camera. Jace didn't blame the reporter one bit. In a pink flowered blouse and pale pink capris, Kitty looked as pretty as the azaleas blooming in the square. Maybe his imagination had gone crazy, but he thought he caught her distinctive rose fragrance mixed with the smells of blooming plants and diesel fuel.

"Here we go." Jace hoisted the colorful pony upward while Ned threaded it into position both above and below.

The camera flashed.

They maneuvered and adjusted until the horse stood proud and handsome beneath the brightly painted roof. He was a polished beauty, his white legs curved in an eternal prance, his pink and turquoise mane flowing backward in a make-believe wind.

"Oh, he's even more beautiful now. Look at him." Kitty clapped again.

Jace stepped back, hands on his hips. "Sweet. Very

sweet." He shook his head. "I still can't believe we've pulled this off."

Kitty playfully whapped his arm. "Pessimist."

He rubbed the spot as if it hurt, drawing a laugh from her.

She'd not missed a beat since that night a week ago in his kitchen. She worked on the project almost every day. She stayed late every night, and if she thought it odd that Jace walked her to her car without trying to kiss her again, she didn't let on.

He'd wanted to. Oh, how he'd wanted to. But he knew what she didn't and that was enough to keep his hands at his sides and his lips to himself.

No one had kissed her since her husband. After all these years of remaining loyal to her husband's memory, why had she chosen him?

Jace's chest expanded, both tormented and thrilled by the knowledge.

He couldn't forget the way she'd felt in his arms or the way she'd softened and melted against him. She was not the kind of woman to do that lightly.

He loved her. He couldn't have her, but like a stray dog, he'd take any crumbs she threw his way.

"Got another box of bulbs for the ladies," Donny stepped upon the circular platform, his focus on Kitty.

Some of Jace's good mood fizzled. Regardless of his good intentions and determination to be more charitable toward Donny, tension gripped him whenever his old cellmate talked to Kitty.

Call it worry. Call it caution. Call it jealousy. The feeling was there, hot and dark and powerful.

Kitty set the carton at her feet next to two others. Both were full. "Thank you."

"Anything for the prettiest lady in town."

On his haunches, Jace unwrapped a glossy black pony and tried to ignore the conversation. Kitty knew Donny found excuses to talk to her. But then, Jace had done the same. Hadn't he orchestrated this moment so he could see Kitty's reaction to the first carousel horses?

From the corner of his eye, he watched Donny fidget as Kitty removed a bulb from the box and went back to work.

"When's this gizmo fire up for riders?" Donny asked.

She took another bulb from the box. "Next weekend. The first night of the Land Run Celebration. I can't wait to see it filled with riders, the lights ablaze and music playing. The park is going to be…like a beautiful fairy tale."

"Oh, it will be. It will be. All because of you." Donny took the bulb from her fingers and stepped closer.

Jace's gut tightened. He paused, listening. Yes, even though he knew Kitty's feelings toward Donny were more compassion than passion, Jace's protective instincts went wild. Kitty's feelings might be platonic. Donny's weren't.

"I can't take the credit. Jace found the carousel."

A smile ballooned in Jace's chest.

"Don't be so modest, Kitty. The idea came from your pretty head." Donny reached for her hand and brought it to his lips. Jace cringed; resentment boiled up in his chest like a tidal wave of heat. "It would be my great honor to escort you to the grand reopening next week."

Kitty's smile faltered. "Well, I—um— You're very sweet to offer."

Okay, that was enough.

Jace dropped the wrench and pushed to his feet. He shouldn't interfere. He should keep his mouth shut.

Jaw tight, he blurted, "Kitty's going with me."

Two faces turned toward him—one annoyed, the other surprised. He was pretty surprised himself. The words had spewed out like an unpredictable geyser. Regardless of his decision to show more trust in Donny, he wasn't about to trust him *that* much. Not with Kitty. She was smart enough to make her own decisions but Jace was taking no chances.

They both knew he hadn't asked her to accompany him anywhere, but he'd wanted to. He braced himself for her denial.

Donny tilted his head, glittery black eyes squinted. "That a fact?"

Jace opened his mouth, hoping something sensible would come out. Before he could speak, Kitty said, "Yes."

A combination of fear and exhilaration shot through him. Later, she'd probably tear his head off for assuming, so he'd better enjoy the moment.

Donny's face darkened but he handled the refusal with grace. "Another time."

He hopped off the platform and strode away.

Jace kept his voice low as he spoke to Kitty. "Am I in trouble?"

"Big trouble." She tried to glare but succeeded only in looking cute.

"You don't have to go with me. I was just—" He shrugged.

"Just what?" She fisted both hands on her hips.

"Being stupid, I guess."

"So, you lied to Donny. You don't want to take me to the celebration?" Her face crumbled. "Now I'm embarrassed."

Oh, man. He'd run his right hand through a router saw before he'd do anything to embarrass Kitty. He was trying to protect her, not hurt her.

"I wasn't sure you'd want to."

"I wasn't sure, either." She bit her bottom lip. "I don't…date."

"Yeah, I know."

"I don't let men kiss me either."

"I know."

Her eyes twinkled. "Not men in general. Just you."

"Yeah?" Jace's stomach dipped, lifted and dipped again.

"Yeah." She cocked her head to one side. "So do you want to take me or not?"

What else could he say?

"I do."

The April night was cool and clear with not a cloud in the sky, a rare treat in Oklahoma's tumultuous spring. The wind, which had been annoying all day, showed her respect for the Land Run Celebration by settling to a soft whisper at sunset.

From the parking area to the far back corner where each fall pecan trees still dripped their seeds into a meandering creek, Redemption Park burgeoned. Street vendors worked out of trailers with such diverse items as sugary funnel cakes and homemade lye soap. Carnival rides were set and ready to run, children already buying their tickets at the booth.

People from all over the state gathered for the two-day festival which had begun at high noon with a thrilling reenactment of the 1889 Land Run.

The citizens of Redemption were in full festival mode, many of them dressed as Kitty was in 19th century garb. She was waiting, along with Jace, the Land Run committee, Ned and dozens of others, for Mayor Frost to make his speech and cut the ribbon on the newly installed carousel.

"Wonder what Opal Banks would have thought of all this?" Jace murmured close to her ear.

Kitty adjusted her hand-crocheted shawl and turned to look at her date. Her stomach jittered. She was on a date. For the first time since she was in high school. All week she'd suffered doubts and more than once, she'd picked up the phone to back out. She'd even prayed that *he* would back out. He hadn't. He'd telephoned twice, both times just to talk. Jace Carter, who seldom strung five sentences together in a day, had called to make small talk.

Kitty was both exhilarated and nervous. Once she'd even gone into the office and talked to Dave's picture, asking his opinion. When Cheyenne, Annie and Sunny had found out about the date, they'd gone into pushy girlfriend mode. They'd done her hair and nails, insisting that nineteenth century women enjoyed manicures.

"Our persnickety Opal would have considered you a most unsuitable rogue." Kitty shook a tiny painted fan under Jace's nose. "And would have swooned in fear of being accosted by such a wild and reckless-looking cowboy."

Jace laughed, smile flashing above the red bandanna tied around his neck.

Somehow during their long phone chats, she'd convinced him to dress as an Old West gunslinger. The result was every bit as good as she'd imagined. In denim pants and leather vest with two day's growth of scruffy beard and a pair of six shooters laced to his thighs he was heart-stoppingly handsome and decidedly dangerous-looking. He'd drawn more than one admiring glance since their arrival at the park, and to her delight, he'd not even noticed.

But she certainly had.

He tipped his chin toward the small, makeshift dais. "Here's the mayor."

"Yea!" She clapped clenched knuckles, her fan wafting a tiny breeze against her warm face. "Finally."

Jace's eyes twinkled down at her. Funny how he didn't have to say a word to make her feel special. All he had to do was look at her with pride and pleasure.

Though reluctant to break eye contact, she turned her attention to the microphone. Mayor Frost and several dignitaries formed a semicircle on the platform. The mayor began his speech, lauding the Land Run Committee for their hard work on the celebration, Kitty for discovering the carousel most people didn't even remember and Jace for his single-minded determination to find the ride once he knew it existed. He went on to praise the workmanship, the volunteer corps and the sense of community generated by one man's dedication.

Beside her Jace fidgeted, unused to compliments. Kitty squeezed his arm, felt humility flowing from him and admired him all the more because of it.

"As you can see the lead horse on the carousel has yet to be unveiled," the mayor said, making a sweeping gesture toward a blanket wrapped pony.

"I hadn't even noticed," Kitty whispered, turning curious eyes to Jace.

Eyes twinkling in a way that told her he knew what

was going on even if she didn't, he shook his head and pointed at Ned who stood on the platform beside the covered pony.

"What?" she whispered. "What is it?"

Jace only shook his head.

"Now if I could," the mayor intoned. "I'd like to have these people join me on the platform, please. Kitty, Chuck and Trina Wainright."

Kitty startled at the mayor's request. Jace's wink told her something was up. He nodded toward the mayor and gave her a gentle push. "Go."

She'd not even realized Trina and Chuck were present, but she saw them coming forward, holding hands. Her heart hammered as she joined them up front.

"Ladies and gentlemen, all of you know that Redemption lost a native son to war. Dave Wainright was a fine man, a good son and husband and a brave soldier."

At the mention of Dave's name, Kitty's throat clogged with tears. Oh, my. Oh, my. What had Jace and Ned done?

"Ned, will you unveil the lead horse please."

Ned, looking self-conscious and anxious and one hundred percent uncertain teenager, slid the blue covering from the animal. Kitty gasped and gripped Trina's hand. The crowd exploded in applause.

A stars and stripes design in vibrant red, white, and blue set the lead pony apart from the others. He was a warrior, a jumper gloriously alive, with proud head high, expression brave as his mane and tail flowed into an imaginary wind. An eagle, wings spread, flew from his breast harness, and the image of an American flag draped beneath the saddle looked real enough to be cloth.

In all the weeks they'd worked on the carousel, she'd never seen this horse.

"He's beautiful," she murmured.

Trina nodded in agreement. "Amazing."

He absolutely was. And so was the man who'd discovered a way to focus Ned's talent. Kitty's gaze found Jace, her gunslinger for the night, grinning proudly from the audience.

When the applause and admiring noises subsided, the mayor continued his speech.

"He's a beauty, all right, a fitting symbol of this carousel's new theme—a permanent and useful exhibit to honor our dedicated men and women in the armed forces. By special request of those who restored the carousel, and with the approval of the town council and the Land Run Committee, I am happy to ask Dave Wainright's family to help me cut the ribbon and then to take the first ride."

Hefting a huge pair of ceremonial scissors, he waited for the three Wainrights to place their hands over his. They were all shaking.

"In honor of David Charles Wainright, I give the citizens of Redemption and future generations the newly named, Hero Carousel."

Kitty hardly felt her hands moving as the ribbon was snipped and she and the Wainrights were honored with the first ride. Tears swam in her eyes. Trina wept openly while Chuck placed an arm over her shoulders and snugged her close.

When the ride was over, her photo had been taken dozens of times, and she'd exchanged hugs with the Wainrights, she stumbled off the platform, knees trembling.

Cheyenne and Trace, Annie and Sloan, and Sunny Case surrounded her. Trina and Chuck joined them. Hugs and pats and congratulations only brought more tears from Trina and Kitty and glassy-eyes from Chuck. Kitty didn't want to cry but this unexpected honor to Dave overwhelmed her.

"This is the nicest thing. Such an honor," she babbled, too emotional to say more.

"Well deserved. A great idea. We're all proud of it."

She looked around at her wonderful circle of close friends. "Did you all know?"

"Of course," Cheyenne said. "The fun and the hard part was keeping you in the dark. You are so nosy."

The group laughed.

Behind them, the carousel opened for business as families climbed aboard and the music began. After a few more minutes of congratulations and conversation, the crowd dispersed, leaving her alone with Jace. Across the way she could see Trina and Chuck surrounded by friends and a reporter. She was fine with that. Let them enjoy the moment. Dave was their son far longer than he was her husband.

The older couple's faces glowed with joy.

"This means so much to them," she said.

"Can't be easy losing a son."

"Their only son. They've never really gotten over his death."

Jace was silent, almost brooding as he watched the carousel circle round and round. She wondered what he was thinking, but didn't ask. She was too excited, too happy. The evening was perfect in many ways. The dedication to Dave, her in-laws' joy and now this time with Jace to explore the feelings growing between them.

"You did this, didn't you?"

He broke out of his reverie, his gaze coming back to settle on her face. "Not by myself."

It was just like Jace to give others the credit, but she knew, and her heart was full with the knowledge that he would do this. Jace Carter was a good, good man.

"Ready to explore the park?" She hooked her hand over his elbow. "I think I hear a cinnamon roll calling my name."

Cinnamon was just one of many scents drifting on the night air. Cotton candy, fried onion burgers, barbecue and funnel cakes warred with each other for attention.

Jace's eyes twinkled. "What? No s'mores?"

Kitty laughed, the bubble of happiness so big she thought she might pop. "The park is full. You never know."

Flirting with Jace was too much fun to resist. They circled the carousel in pursuit of sensational cinnamon delights, passing men wearing ten-gallon hats and six-guns and ladies in bustles or prairie bonnets. The festive, Old West atmosphere added to her enjoyment.

Trina and Chuck stood talking to friends. As Kitty passed by, she caught Trina's gaze and smiled. Trina's eyes flashed to where Kitty gripped Jace's elbow. Her face froze in shock before she turned and said something to Chuck. Then they both frowned in Kitty's direction.

Kitty's spirits plummeted. Her step faltered. Jace slowed his pace, looked down at her with a questioning gaze. "What's wrong?"

She shook her head, lips pressed together. She shouldn't feel ashamed and yet she did.

When she didn't answer, Jace looked around. He must have seen Trina and Chuck. "Do you want to go talk to them?"

"No." What would she say? "I don't want to ruin their evening."

Jace's jaw tightened. "And you think your being with me would ruin their evening?"

"I'm sorry."

The light in his hazel eyes dimmed. "If you want me to leave, I will."

Chapter Fifteen

Jace held his breath, both angry and hurt. He had no right to be, had promised himself not to read anything into tonight, but his heart wouldn't listen.

He'd believed Kitty cared for him and had even entertained the insane hope that he could find a way to hide his past from her forever.

Lacquer fumes must have gone to his head.

Kitty puffed out a hard breath. "Jace, I—" She huffed again. "I don't know what to do sometimes. Could we talk about this?"

He pointed toward the cinnamon bun vendor. A half-dozen picnic tables had been set up around the popular booth. "Let's grab a roll and sit down."

After buying the rolls and coffee, they chose an unoccupied table and sat. He didn't hold out much hope that they would be alone for long, but this would do for starters.

With the smell of cinnamon and hot butter driving

him crazier than he already was, he said, "They don't approve."

"That's putting it mildly." She tore off a chunk of the warm bread and fiddled with it. "Trina and Chuck love me. I love them. I don't want them hurt."

All right, he was a man. He could handle her rejection here and now. He'd been expecting her to come to her senses, and it was only fitting the rejection should come tonight. If she chose a dead man's memory over him, so be it. He would go back to where he'd been before he'd loved her. He'd be safe again and never have to worry about her finding out the truth. Short-term pain was easier than her knowing.

"They've lost a lot," he said. "They deserve your affection."

"That's the thing, see?" Troubled, she twisted the chunk of roll. "They lost the most important person in their lives, and I'm their last link to Dave. Since his death, I've carried the torch, so to speak."

"I thought you wanted to."

"I did. I loved Dave, Jace. He was this town's hero. He was my hero, and keeping his memory fresh and alive has been an honor. I've loved every trinket I've painted, every eagle pencil I've sold, every photo or poster hanging in my office."

The stab he'd expected at her admission of love for Dave didn't transpire. Instead, he was proud of her. Doing the right thing was Kitty's way and one of the reasons Jace had fallen in love with her. Besides, how could a man be jealous of a dead hero?

"He deserved that."

"Yes, he did." She fidgeted, put the roll down, picked the coffee up but set it down, too. Jace remained silent, aware that all he could do was listen. The ball really was in her court.

"I'm thirty-one years old and all of a sudden the rest of my life seems too long to be a widow. I don't know what happened to me. I used to be content with my motel and my memories." She lifted tormented blue eyes to his. "Am I terrible for wanting to spend time with you?"

The rhythm of his heartbeat changed. Dread lifted. Suddenly, he could breathe again.

"I hope not." *He* was terrible for wanting to be with *her,* but she could never be anything but wonderful. "You've been good to them, Kitty. You always will be. That's who you are, but you have to decide how to spend your life. You can't let someone else decide."

"That's what everyone says."

"What matters is what *you* say."

Her smile returned. She drew in a breath that lifted the leg-of-mutton shoulders of her Victorian dress. The satiny blue material rustled. "Then I say we finish these rolls and do what we came here to do."

"And what was that?"

"Have some fun."

He wasn't about to argue.

The rest of the evening was a dream Jace would remember the rest of his life. He was with the woman he loved and she seemed happy to be with him.

Amidst the noise and bustle, the music and food Jace did everything he could to insure she had a good time. He bought her cotton candy and had their picture taken in an Old West setting. He stood behind, one hand on her shoulder and tried to look serious, although Kitty said something silly and he laughed. She sat in front, her skirt fluffed around her, flirtatiously waving her fan. He'd paid sixty dollars to capture a moment he would treasure forever.

Later, with guns blazing, he'd come to the rescue when a band of mock outlaws rushed the crowded bandstand and took "the widow woman" captive. He rode the colorful, light-festooned Ferris wheel and showed her the whole of Redemption from the top. She'd squealed and gripped his arm in a display of playful terror. They even tried a turn at square dancing, laughing hard to discover neither had a lick of rhythm.

By the time he took her home, physically weary but emotionally full, midnight approached.

"Want to come in?" Kitty asked when he took her key and opened the door.

"Better not. It's late."

"Okay."

Yet, they lingered in the open doorway, with the soft yellow light from inside bathing them in a shadowy glow. She, a respected lady in her rustling blue dress and he in outlaw gear seemed ironically appropriate.

"Jace." She reached for his hand.

"What?" Her fingers curled in his, small and cool.

"I was just thinking."

He tilted his head. "About?"

"You. Me. Us."

"Is there an us?"

Her teeth caught her bottom lip, her blue eyes large as she nodded. "I think so. Don't you?"

"Yes." Despite the warnings clanging in his head, he couldn't resist. He'd been too long without love in his life. Too long since anyone cared for him on a personal level. A man could be thirsty only so long.

Head down, she played with his fingers, opening and closing each one. "You don't sound too happy."

"I don't deserve someone like you." He forced a smile. "You're the most special woman I've ever known."

"Oh, Jace," she murmured on a sigh. "I'm scared and happy and—"

"I feel the same." For different reasons.

"Being with you is—" She dropped his hand, clutched a fist to her heart. "Like I can breathe again. Like I'm alive again."

"I know." He rested his forehead against hers. "I know."

"I was thinking…"

His lips curved. "About?"

"Maybe you should kiss me."

His heart jumped but he teased, "Is that all you think about?"

Laughing softly, she tiptoed up, slid her arms

around his neck, and rocked his world. "I'm falling in love with you."

And then she kissed him.

Jace arrived home, his head reeling. Hope and fear and wonder flowed through him like shock waves. Tonight was the best night of his life. Kitty was falling in love with him.

He removed his Old West gear and hung the costume neatly in the closet. Maybe he'd wear the rig again next year with Kitty at his side.

She loved him.

His heart had almost burst out of his chest when she'd said those words. He'd pulled her close and breathed in her soft rose scent, thanking God and fighting the inner demons that threatened everything.

Anything he did now would hurt her. If he walked away without an explanation, she'd be hurt. If he told her the truth, she'd be hurt. Which was the lesser of the evils?

He closed his eyes, head back, hands on his hips. "Lord Jesus, what do I do now?"

Milo heard him and lifted his head from the foot of the air mattress. The dog made small wrinkles on the otherwise perfectly made bed.

"Hey, little buddy. Just talking to God here. Go back to sleep."

As if the pup understood, he snuggled into the sheets and closed his eyes.

Jace stripped off his shirt and wadded it into a ball, which he aimed toward the laundry basket in the corner of the bare room. He needed some furniture.

Still vacillating between worry and wonder, he didn't hear the footsteps coming down the hall. The first indication that he was no longer alone came with the sound of Ned's horrified voice.

"Dude." The word was a stunned breath. "What happened to you?"

Jace whipped around with the speed of light, grappling for the discarded shirt behind him. "What are you doing in here?"

"I found something in Donny's room, I—" Ned gulped, eyes wide as he stared at Jace in horrified curiosity. "Man, I never seen nothing like that. Somebody slice you up?"

Jace knew what the teen had seen. The lattice work of keloid scars on his shoulder, side and back still made him flinch. He couldn't imagine how revolting the scars looked to someone else.

He shoved his arms into the retrieved shirt, yanked the front together and buttoned it. His fingers shook, infuriating him. What right did Ned have to come inside this room without warning? And why hadn't he shut the door? The last time he'd seen either of his houseguests, they'd still been at the park.

"You keep this to yourself. A man's got a right to privacy."

Ned took the offensive. "Like, who am I gonna tell?"

They glared at each other for two beats before Ned shrugged again. "I'm going to bed."

He spun away, hurt and anger flowing from him like heat.

"Wait."

Ned paused in the doorway but didn't turn. "I don't want to impose on your precious privacy."

The sarcastic tone belied his hurt.

Jace blew out a shaky breath. God, what a mess.

"You couldn't know. You didn't do anything wrong."

Ned slowly turned, hovered, half boy, half adult, not worldly wise enough to know what to say. Jace felt like a jerk. The only person he'd been concerned about was himself.

"I'm oversensitive about the—scars. No big deal. Forget it." *Please* forget it. Forget you came in here. Forget what you saw.

"So you gonna tell me what happened?"

So much for forgetting.

He'd never told a soul, never discussed the incident with anyone after the fact. But here stood Ned, needy and curious and concerned. He'd already seen. He might as well know.

"Just between me and you?"

"That bad?"

"Worse."

"I ain't talking. You can count on me."

He knew that. In the time since Ned had come into his life, the surly, troubled kid had shown his true colors in the workshop. Some people would call him crazy, but Jace trusted Ned implicitly. He, more than anyone, knew the boy had changed.

"Want some coffee or something?"

"Nah, too late."

"Pull up a corner of my mattress and I'll tell you a bedtime story guaranteed to give you nightmares. It does me."

Ned snorted but joined Jace on the edge of the air bed. He rested his elbows on his tall, jean-clad knees and let his hands dangle. He was still a bundle of self-consciousness, unsure of what to do with all those arms and legs.

"You ever done anything you wished you could take back?"

Ned slanted a glance at him. "I been busted twice. What do you think?"

Jace chuffed softly. "Me, too. More than twice."

"You? No way. You're a Jesus dude."

"Jesus is the reason I'm still breathing. Jesus and a man named Gary who saw something worth saving in a kid with a bad attitude. No one could tell me anything. I got involved with a gang. The badder I was, the bigger man I was."

"Yeah, I know about that stuff. It's a crock."

Yes, the boy had come a long way.

"I wish I'd been half as smart as you are, but I wasn't. I got busted big time. Armed robbery. Being barely eighteen, everyone said I would walk. I didn't."

"No kidding? Man, that stinks. How long?"

"Three years."

Ned whistled through his teeth. "Brutal."

The kid had no idea how brutal.

Milo, disturbed by the whistle, inched forward and flopped his head on Jace's thigh. He rubbed the soft ears, taking comfort in the sweetness of the puppy.

"Prison's a lousy place, especially for the young and halfway decent-looking. I was scared to death." He didn't want to go into detail but Ned was smart enough to figure out the rest. A teenager in a prison full of hardened criminals was a target.

"That where you got cut up?"

"Everyone was in a gang in prison. Everyone. A few other younger guys and me banded together for protection. We tried to outbad the bad. Wrong move. I made enemies of some bad people."

"They jumped you?"

"In the shower." He shuddered at the memory of a hand grabbing his hair, yanking him back with a cruel grunt of laughter. He'd whirled around, fists flying. He'd seen the homemade knife flash and warded off the first few jabs, though his hands had been sliced. He glanced down at them now, saw the scars others blamed on working with saws. He'd always let them believe what they wanted.

"One had a knife. I fought like a tiger until three of them slammed me onto the concrete." His voice faded. Milo opened one eye, eyebrow arched. "They held me down, stood on my hands so I couldn't fight.

Torres sat on my back, held my head. I knew I was a dead man."

Memories flashed behind his eyes of his own red blood swirling down the drain as water beat from the showers and Torres sliced him into hamburger meat. He never knew if he'd screamed or cried but he recalled Torres's laugh, cruel and triumphant. And he remembered the starbursts of agony.

"What happened?"

"I must have passed out because I don't remember any of this, but apparently Donny was passing the showers, heard something and alerted the guards." He scrubbed both hands over his face. "Next day I woke up in the hospital with about a million stitches in my body. The wounds got infected. The scars turned ugly. But I survived, thanks to Donny."

"Now I get why you let him hang around."

"Wouldn't you? He saved my worthless life."

"That's why you let me work for you, too, isn't it? I mean, you know." He studied his long hands. "I was on the same path as you."

Jace liked hearing Ned use the past tense. He'd done plenty of praying that this kid would not end up the way he had. "Partly. I needed your help, too."

"I get that. Tonight was cool." He rocked a little, showing his pleasure in the night's events. "We did good."

"Yeah, we did."

"What did Miss Wainright think of my horse?

His expression was eager but uncertain. Ned needed lots of positive input but he was gaining ground.

"She cried."

He tossed his hair to one side. "Sweet."

Jace chuckled. Remembering the carousel made him feel less worthless. "You like making ladies cry?"

Ned hiked a shoulder, grinning, the once surly eyes alight. "Maybe. So, you in love with her, or what?"

All the air rushed out of Jace. How did the conversation turn from the miserable topic of prison to the exhilarating, uncomfortable topic of love?

"Yeah, wise guy. I am." Jace punched Ned lightly on the knee. "Keep that to yourself, too."

"Come on, man. She's gotta know. A woman like that, all sweet and nice. You can't let her get away."

Jace dropped his head. "I got a record, Ned. She's a hero's widow."

Ned shifted around, pinned him with a stare. "You think that matters to her?"

Heaviness settled in Jace's chest. "It should. She deserves better."

"Dude, I don't know. Don't seem right. What are you going to do?"

"Same thing I've always done. Nothing." But could he go back to nothing now? After what she'd said to him tonight?

"What about her? Don't she get a say?"

"Think about what I just told you, Ned. Do you ~ink I want her to know the truth about me?"

"But you ain't that man anymore. You're—" His shoulders went up. "You're a good guy. Everyone likes you."

"They like who they think I am. A man's reputation is a fragile thing. Takes years to build. Seconds to destroy. I can't chance it."

"All right. I get what you're saying. But why'd you tell me all this?"

He wasn't really sure. Maybe he'd simply needed to tell someone. And Ned had seen the scars. He'd asked.

"I don't trust very many people. But I trust you."

"I won't let you down."

"I know that."

Ned suddenly jerked as if he'd been shocked and then leaped to his feet. "Dude, I nearly forgot. I gotta talk to you about something."

Jace's heart plummeted. After all this talk, was the kid in trouble again?

He returned the sleeping puppy to his favorite spot and stood, too. Ned was pacing, clearly agitated.

"What's wrong? Did something happen at the festival?"

"No, nothing like that." He fidgeted, glanced out the opened door and back again. "Well, see, when I got home, I thought Donny was here. I went in his room to tell him something and—" He hesitated, eyes sliding away to look at the sleeping puppy. "Don't get mad, but when he wasn't there, I kind of nosed around."

What could he say? He'd done the same.

"And?"

"His computer was on. I kinda looked at his files."

"Kinda?"

"I know. I shouldn't have but sometimes I don't trust him much."

"We have that in common. I don't always trust him either. But he saved my life."

"Well, that's the thing. We shouldn't trust him. He's up to something, Jace."

Jace tensed, on full alert, his fears tumbling in like a landslide. "Like what?"

"I'm no businessman, but it looks like shady dealings. Want to look for yourself?"

As if he had a choice. "You don't open a can of worms and then walk away."

Jace followed Ned to Donny's bedroom, leery of what he would find. The room was messy, something that bothered Jace enough to stay out of it. Donny's laptop was closed but the light indicated the power was on. Ned opened the lid and tapped the finger pad, then scrolled through files, opening several.

Jace bent over the screen, watching. "You looked at all these?"

Shamefaced, Ned nodded, but made no excuse. "Look at this one. That's Miss Wainright's name and information and something about the motel's assets and tax returns."

Jace went on red alert, reading rapidly. If Kitty had

invested with Donny, she'd never mentioned the fact to him. The papers were legal documents with land descriptions and loan information and gross assets—Kitty's. There was other business mumbo jumbo that he didn't begin to comprehend. The file that worried him most was a spreadsheet.

"There's a whole list of names here. With stars and numbers by several. Wonder what it means?"

"You got me. Maybe it's legit."

"Maybe." But Jace was taking no chances. That was Kitty's information in there. "Can you run this off or email it to my computer without Donny knowing?"

Ned grinned and wiggled his fingers. "What do you think? Let me at that keyboard."

In seconds, four files had been emailed to Jace's computer. He didn't know what any of them meant. Maybe nothing at all, but he wanted a good long look without the worry of Donny walking in.

"Put everything back the way it was. If he's up to something, I don't want him to get suspicious."

"Just like on TV."

Jace grunted. TV wasn't near as scary as reality.

Chapter Sixteen

At sunup, Jace awoke with grit in his eyes and dread in his gut, having barely slept at all. Long after Ned had ambled off to bed, Jace remained awake, reading Donny's files. When he'd finally collapsed, exhausted next to Milo, he'd tossed and turned until the little dog had given up and left the room.

He figured he should feel guilty about the serious invasion of Donny's privacy, but he didn't. Not yet anyway.

He'd learned little from the documents, but then he wasn't into real estate investments. He built houses. He didn't sell them. He knew next to nothing about returns on investments or portfolios. But he knew someone who might.

He was in his truck on his way to see Sloan Hawkins when his cell phone jingled. Kitty's name flashed on the screen.

Jace's pulse quickened. "'Morning."

"Good morning yourself." Her sweet, cheerful

voice made him smile. "Did I dream this or did we have a great time last night?"

"The best."

"And not a s'more in sight."

"Must have been the cinnamon rolls."

"Or the cotton candy."

"Or the candied apple."

"Ugh." She laughed softly. "I think I have serious sweet tooth."

That wasn't the only sweet thing about her. He glanced down at the copied files lying beside him.

"Kitty, this may sound crazy but I need to ask you something."

"Okay."

"Did you invest any money into Donny's business?"

"He discussed it with me, but no, I haven't. Trina did and she got a nice return. Why? Are you thinking of investing, too?"

Not a chance. "Just wondering."

Donny was dirty. Jace's insides cringed. He'd suspected all along, but now he knew. There was no good reason for Donny to have Kitty's financial information in his computer files. Somehow, he'd dragged Kitty's name into whatever he was doing. As tempted as Jace was to discuss the situation with Kitty, he wouldn't. Not until he knew more. No use scaring her half to death.

The line hummed and Jace searched for something to distract them both. "What are you doing today?"

"Actually, that's why I called. Would you like to have lunch later? And maybe take in the art and crafts show at town hall?"

More than anything, though caution said to stay clear. After last night's reminder of his past and this morning's reminder that the past would follow him and cause trouble for the people he loved, he had no business being with Kitty.

"I'm kind of busy this morning."

"Oh. Well." The disappointment came through loud and clear.

Call him a sucker, but he hated for Kitty to be disappointed. "I think I can squeeze in lunch."

"You can? I'd love that. Noon. Here at my house?"

"No man can resist a home cooked meal. What are you feeding me?"

"Gourmet surprise."

"Now I'm scared."

She laughed. "S'mores, cotton candy and cinnamon rolls."

"I'm all over that."

They both chuckled, lingering a bit longer to say silly, nonsensical things that people in love said just to hear the other's voice.

Was she really in love with him?

Listening to her sweet voice, he steered the truck through town where city workers were sweeping up last night's celebration. Popbottle Jones and GI Jack were already on the job, gathering leftovers. They raised their hands in greeting as he passed.

"Well, I have to go," she said. "One of last night's customers is ready to check out."

The motel had been filled to capacity yesterday with most of the clients remaining in town for the weekend. Jace felt good that the major repairs had been finished on time, even though he'd not done some of them. If not for good old Harvey running the office, Kitty couldn't have attended the festivities last night.

Donny had run the office, too—on the day she'd picnicked with Jace.

A slow anger began to build. If Donny Babcock had done anything to hurt Kitty…

"See you at noon." He started to hang up.

"Jace."

He returned the receiver to his ear. "Yes?"

"Last night was the best time I've had in a long time." Then the line went silent, leaving his heart full and his stomach churning with worry.

She'd soon know he'd brought trouble to her doorstep. What would she think then?

Kitty hummed a merry tune as she thought of last night and of the lunch to come. Jace made her heart sing.

The carousel dedication had blessed her immeasurably, but it was the time with Jace that had filled her dreams.

She'd never laughed so much or felt as important as she did when she was with him. And the way he kissed her.

Her belly kerplopped. Oh, my. There was such tender restraint, such reverence in the way he touched her.

"Lord, I love him. I didn't know before but now I do. I love him."

Before she could move forward with their relationship, she had to talk to Trina and Chuck. Though she dreaded the meeting, their feelings mattered.

At nine, she closed the office and hung a sign on the door, declaring her intention to return in an hour. Dear Harvey was still asleep and all her customers had paid with a credit card. If they checked out while she was gone, she'd know when she returned.

Maybe she wasn't a very good businesswoman, but the motel had occupied enough of her time. Life was out there waiting. Life and love and a future she wanted more than she'd ever dreamed.

Ten minutes later, she was seated in the Wainrights' sage green living room, sipping fragrant lemon tea she really didn't want. Dave's photos lined the fireplace mantel, the walls, the end tables. The Wainright home was every bit as much of a shrine as the motel office.

Touched with a newfound compassion, Kitty prayed to handle the coming conversation with the grace and love the Wainrights deserved.

"Where's Chuck this morning?"

Trina waved a hand. "On the volunteer clean-up crew downtown."

"Nice of him."

Trina leaned forward to set her teacup on the coffee table. "Wasn't the carousel dedication a wonderful surprise?"

"It was." Kitty fidgeted with a sugar spoon.

Please, Lord don't let them be hurt any more than they already are.

"Dave would be honored. A little embarrassed at all the attention, but he would have appreciated the sentiment."

The sugar spoon clinked against china as Kitty straightened and drew in a calming breath.

"Trina, that's what I wanted to talk to you about."

"The dedication?"

"No, about Dave."

"Okay."

Regardless of the lemon tea, her mouth had gone dry. She licked her lips. "I loved Dave. I was a good wife to him."

"Yes, you were, honey." Trina patted her hand.

Kitty twisted a napkin, laid it aside, and noticed her fingers were shaking. She gripped them together in her lap.

"I love you and Chuck and if what I'm about to say hurts you, I'm sorry."

Trina's soft expression tightened. "This is about that Carter boy, isn't it?"

She didn't bother to correct her former mother-in-law, though Jace was hardly a boy.

"Yes." She swallowed the lump of nerves. "I'm in love with him."

As she'd expected, tears gathered in Trina's eyes. Her cheeks blotched red. "Don't be silly, Kitty. You can't be."

"I'm a grown woman, Trina, not a child. I know my heart, and my heart loves Jace."

The woman she'd considered a mother since high school changed before her eyes. Her mouth tightened. Her eyes narrowed and shot arrows of anger.

"How can you do this to us? How can you cheat on Dave? You have no right. You're his wife."

The accusation cut like a knife but Kitty resisted the urge to argue. Trina and Chuck had been hurt enough, and she was hurting them again, though unintentionally. Desperate to handle this the Christian way, she fought not to say anything she might regret.

"Dave is gone, Trina. I'm sorry if you don't understand, but I'm a young woman alone who needs to love and be loved. I need to have a life."

"And you think Jace Carter loves you?" Trina's lips curled with disdain. "What do you even know about him?"

"I know how good he is to me. I know he orchestrated the carousel dedication to please me and to bless you. And I know how I feel when I'm with him."

"He's just using you."

"Why would he do that? Please, Trina, let's don't do this. I love you. I don't want to fight." Kitty's heart beat with such force, she felt the pain of it in her throat. "I don't want to disrespect Dave's memory but I am going to be with Jace."

"You're being foolish and you'll end up humiliated and broke. Jace Carter doesn't love you. He loves what you own. He wants your property and your monthly check from Dave's pension. Why else would he spend so much time working on that motel? Oh, honey, I'm saying this for your own good. Don't be fooled by the first handsome man to whisper in your ear."

Lord help her. Like a fist to the stomach, the hurt jabbed deep and took her breath. But she was not going to dignify such nonsense with a rebuttal.

Kitty stood, knees trembling and voice shaky. Tears pushed at the back of her throat.

"Jace Carter is a fine man and I love him. And he loves me. I have absolutely no doubt of that." She gripped her purse like a lifeline, holding tight to keep from flying into a million pieces. "I'm going home, Trina, and I'm not coming back. You are welcome to come to me if you choose and I will forgive the terrible things you just said to me. I love you. I always will."

The older woman put her face in her hands and wept.

With all the dignity she could muster, Kitty let herself out of the house she'd considered a second home. Once in the car, she let the tears come.

* * *

"So my instincts were right all along?"

Jace was about as sick to his stomach as he could get without throwing up. He was inside the Hawkinses' mansion, as some people still called the rambling Victorian, in Sloan's office. From this room of telephone lines, computers and high-tech machinery, Sloan owned and operated Worldwide Security Solutions, a crackerjack team that did everything from protecting rare museum exhibits to guarding high ranking officials around the globe. His expertise in law enforcement and general knowledge about crime and criminals wasn't exactly what Jace needed, but it was a start.

"Looks that way. Can't be sure yet, but I have a friend in the SEC. He'll check it out for us."

"The SEC? You think this is security fraud?"

"We'll soon know." He handed Jace a list of names they'd taken from Donny's files. All except a handful were Redemption residents.

"I'll call Wes and get him on it. You call these people, find out what you can without alarming anyone."

Over the next hour, they both made telephone calls. With each one, Jace's hopes sank lower and Donny's game became clearer. Then Sloan's friend in the SEC returned the call and confirmed their worst suspicions. Donny was running an investment scam, a clever type of Ponzi scheme. His operation was small scale, based on relationships and lies and false documents, but a scam that would rob honest people nonetheless.

"Sorry, Jace. This looks bad."

Jace groaned. Guilt ripped him. "All these people trusted him because of me. Every last person I spoke with said they'd invested with Donny because he told them I'd invested. I was his friend. They could trust him. And they'd fallen for it." He ground his teeth. "Because of me."

"Fortunately, he's still on the ground floor and hasn't done much damage yet. Most of the people haven't invested all that much. A few thousand here and there."

"That's a lot of money to a retiree." The old Jace reared his ugly head. "I could break his neck and not regret it."

"Easy, buddy. You gotta be smart about this."

Sloan's phone beeped and he answered, speaking into a headpiece. As he listened, his complexion darkened, his blue gaze clouded.

As if he wasn't already about to implode, Jace got a very bad feeling.

"What is it?" he asked as soon as Sloan said goodbye.

"You're not going to be happy."

"It can't get much worse."

"Yes, it can. He used Kitty's motel as collateral on a very large loan. I seriously doubt she knows anything about it."

All the blood drained from Jace's head. His brain pounded. "She doesn't. I asked her this morning."

The red haze cleared and he pushed to his feet. Desperate to get his hands on Donny, he bolted toward his truck, heedless of Sloan's voice calling him back.

GI Jack sopped thick, white gravy with one of Miriam Martinelli's fat golden biscuits and listened to the talk flowing around the table inside the Sugar Shack. He smacked his lips and allowed a little moan of appreciation. Nobody made biscuits like Miriam.

The Sugar Shack was packed as always but today as much with tourists as regulars. Tooney Deer, Doc Bowman, Deputy Jessie Rainwater, and local firefighter Zak Ashford had all pulled up chairs for a bite to eat and a jolt of caffeine and conversation. They were lauding the Land Run festivities when Sloan Hawkins stormed in, looking dark and deadly. GI Jack wasn't scared of much, but if he was ever in an alley fight, he wanted Sloan Hawkins on his side.

"Ahoy, Sloan." GI waved a biscuit to get his attention.

Sloan frowned around the room, scoping out everyone in the place before he stalked toward his friends' table. Without preliminaries, he said, "Any of you seen Donny Babcock today?"

"Can't say I have. How about you fellers?" Heads

wagged all around the table. "Why? Something wrong?"

"I'm going to find out." With that curious comment, he turned on his boot heel, silver chain jangling against his ankle, and exited the Sugar Shack.

"Sure feel sorry for Babcock if he's stirred that hornet's nest," Jessie Rainmaker said.

The rest of them chuckled and went back to their food. Five minutes later, Donny Babcock entered the building.

"Well, looky here."

Tooney chuckled. "He's still alive. Guess Hawkins didn't find him."

Curious as to what was going on—a nosy trait he never denied—GI Jack waved him over. "Pull up a chair, son. Take a load off."

Donny flashed the set of teeth GI Jack was convinced were false and hollered at Sassy Carlson to bring him a soda.

"Gorgeous day today."

"That it is. Did you run into Sloan Hawkins? He was in here earlier looking for you."

"He was?" Donny accepted his soda from Sassy with a wink. Immune to flirty men, Sassy patted his shoulder and left. "I wonder what he wanted."

"Didn't say, but he didn't look happy."

"Hmm. Interesting. Hawkins and I got no business dealings. I barely know the man."

"Speaking of business, Donny." Tooney's spoon clinked against the table. He leaned back against the lattice-backed chair. "Jace Carter called this morning asking questions about our investment deal. You said he was your partner and all, but I thought he was a silent partner."

Donny's skin blanched. GI Jack wouldn't normally have noticed but something didn't feel right. Hadn't felt right since Sloan stormed in and out like a thunderclap. The air had that eerie, about-to-come-a-tornado, feeling. This time, the tornado might be of human creation.

"Jace called you? That *is* odd. I'll have to ask him about it."

"Called me, too," Doc Bowman said. "I told him I hadn't invested. Cheyenne and I are still praying about it."

"Well, friend, don't pray too long. You know what they say about good deals. Get in, or get left out." Donny pushed back from the table, taking his soft drink with him. "Good seeing all of you."

As he left, GI Jack exchanged glances with Pop-bottle Jones. His friend nodded in silent agreement. Something was up.

After fifteen minutes of pouring her broken heart out to God, Kitty had drawn in a shaky breath, washed her face, and started something she should have done years ago. Her stomach ached and her head hurt, but her heart was at peace. She'd made the right decision.

Slowly, she moved through the office taking down

old photos to stack neatly into a plastic storage bin. Dave's face smiled out at her, encouraging, reassuring. He'd always wanted the best for her. Why hadn't she realized that he, more than anyone, would never have wanted her to build a shrine and hide in it?

She was dusting the folded flag that had draped his coffin when the bell over the office door jingled and Donny Babcock strode in. He stopped when he saw what she was doing.

"No offense, Kitty, but it's about time."

Her smile was tremulous. "Yes."

He came around behind the counter, though she'd not invited him. He took the flag from her hands and set it on the counter. He seemed more fidgety today than usual, his eyes darted here and there, his shoulders tweaking at intervals.

"I need to speak with you. It's urgent."

"Is everything all right?"

He didn't answer. Instead he reached for her hand. Kitty pulled away. The action brought a scowl to Donny's face.

"You must know I have feelings for you, Kitty. Forgive me if I'm too bold, but I'm in love with you. Will you marry me? I'm leaving today on business and want you to go with me. The Caribbean is beautiful this time of year."

The shocking invitation came out of nowhere.

"Donny, I had no idea. I—" Her hand went to her aching head. "I can't. I'm sorry. I can't."

Donny's expression hardened. "It's Jace, isn't it?"

"Yes."

"Oh, Kitty." He shook his head. "My poor, sweet, innocent love. I wanted to spare you this. I tried. Lord knows I tried. But he fooled you, too."

"What are talking about? Jace is the most honest man I know."

"Oh? Well, that relieves my mind. As long as you know the truth, you can make your own choices."

Kitty blinked, bewildered. "The truth about what?"

Sympathy poured off Donny. He patted her shoulder and very gently said, "About his—" He bit his lip, looked away, reluctant. "Surely he told you about his past."

"I'm not sure what you're referring to." Jace had grown up in the city, gone to school there and learned his trade. His mother had raised him and he'd mourned the lack of a father. He'd lived in Redemption for years, been a friend to her for all that time. What else was there to know?

Donny paced away, looked out the office window and turned, hands on his hips, jacket flared. "It breaks my heart to be the one to tell you. But I can't let you go on believing a lie."

"What are you talking about? Just tell me."

"Promise not to hate me. I never meant for you to be hurt in all this."

"All of what? Please, Donny, you're starting to scare me."

"All right, but remember, this was not my idea. I

never wanted to see you hurt." He paused, the moment full of tension that added to the ache in Kitty's head. "Jace Carter is a hardened criminal. He spent three years in Lexington Prison for a violent armed robbery. It wasn't his first nor his last. He came to this little burg to hide and do his dirty work over and over again."

Ripples of shock raised the hair on her neck. "I don't believe you."

"Believe it, my darling lady. I would never lie to you. You are too precious to me. Jace learned the building trade in prison. Those scars on his hands? A knife fight that almost took his life. Jace is a criminal, Kitty." He pulled a badge from his jacket. "I didn't want you to know, but I'm a U.S. Marshal, under-cover, sent to bring him in."

"This is insane." But the badge looked real.

Donny's cell phone rang. He turned it off.

"I can see how much you care for him. I have a heart, Kitty. My love for you—" He paused, touched his heart in a dramatic gesture of love and pain. "My love for you makes me want to do something crazy to spare you this heartache and embarrassment."

"I thought you were friends."

"I've become fond of him, that's true. But it's you I care about, Kitty."

Kitty slid onto a chair, shocked and confused. Was Donny telling the truth? He couldn't be. He couldn't be. "I need to call Jace."

"No, dear lady, you can't. You mustn't." Donny's

voice was a syrupy monotone, soothing as if he feared she'd fly to pieces. He didn't know her very well. "You need to listen to me. I can help you. I can help him."

"How?"

"He needs money to get out of town. Mexico would be the best place for him to go right now."

The banging in her head grew louder. She couldn't think straight. Nothing made sense. "I don't want him to leave."

"Do you want to see him in prison?"

"No. But if what you say is true, helping him escape would be wrong." Pain shot between her eyebrows. She thought she might throw up. "I'm not doing anything until I talk to Jace."

Donny blew out an exasperated sigh.

"I tried. Remember that. I tried. And now I am forced to do my job and bring him in." He kissed her on the cheek. "Goodbye, sweet lady."

The moment he exited the building, Kitty rushed into the bathroom and was violently ill.

Chapter Seventeen

He couldn't find Donny anywhere. And the creep wouldn't answer his cell phone.

In the hours since discovering Donny's treachery, Jace had driven and called until the boiling rage had eased to a simmer. In a way, he was glad he hadn't found Donny yet. He might have done something more criminal than armed robbery. Silently, he thanked the Lord for watching out for him.

"Help me find him before he gets wind of the investigation and takes off."

He wasn't sure what he would do when he found Donny but he hoped to get the truth. Maybe it wasn't too late to recoup the money his friends had invested.

He circled around for one more pass through town. With the Land Run Celebration winding down today, the streets were crowded. Donny liked lights and noise and people. He could be hidden among the revelers.

With a sigh, Jace rubbed the bridge of his nose.

His cell phone rang. With a jolt, he saw Kitty's name flash across the screen and checked the time. In all the turmoil of the morning, he'd almost forgotten their lunch date.

As much as he wanted to be with her, he dreaded the conversation they'd have, but at some point she needed to know what Donny had done. And what he'd done as well.

"Hello."

"Jace?" Her voice sounded weird.

He sat up straighter. "Are you okay?"

"No. Jace." She took a shaky breath. "Is it true what Donny said?"

Fear crawled up Jace's throat and threatened to strangle him. "Have you talked to Donny? Where is he?"

"He's looking for you. He said…he said…" Her voice broke.

Jace's hand tightened on the wheel. "Did the creep tell you about the motel?"

He'd wanted to be with her when she heard the news, to hold her and promise that he'd do everything he could to protect her business from financial ruin.

"The motel? I don't know what you mean."

With his attention on Kitty, Jace almost missed the stop sign at the corner of Main and Mercy. Not wanting to add an accident to his growing list of worries, he pulled into a space alongside the Town Square and put the truck in idle.

"Let's start again. Tell me what's wrong."

"Donny said you'd been in prison. He said you were a criminal. I know he was lying. Please tell me he was lying."

Jace's world imploded. He leaned his forehead on the steering wheel and wondered why he hadn't died on that concrete floor. Why had God let him live?

"Jace? Jace? Talk to me. It isn't true, is it?"

He did the only honest thing left to do. He said, "Yes, it is," and hung up the phone.

A million regrets rushed through him. He should have told her long ago. He should never have broken his vow to keep a neutral distance. He should never have kissed her, never have let her love him.

With a groan ripped from his churning belly, he banged his head against the hard plastic.

She wouldn't love him now.

Jace didn't know how long he remained with his head on the steering wheel, mourning and praying, but a tap on the window jerked him upright.

Popbottle Jones and GI Jack stood beside his truck, concern on their weathered faces. He rolled the window down, too disheartened to say hello.

"Trouble, Jace Carter?"

"I'm okay."

"Strange place for an afternoon nap."

Jace allowed a humorless twitch of lips. "Bad day."

"We figured as much." Popbottle Jones leaned

an elbow on the rearview mirror. His suit coat, the color of pumpkins, was torn at the cuff. "Your trouble wouldn't have anything to do with that loquacious friend of yours, Donny Babcock?"

Jace sighed. These two men got around town. They noticed and knew things most people didn't. "He's running an investment scam."

GI Jack's head bobbed up and down. "We heard that rumor. Hoped it wasn't true."

"It is," Jace said grimly.

"Since we're clarifying rumors, let me ask you something personal. Are you involved?"

Jace jerked. "No."

"As we suspected, more of Mr. Babcock's fabrication. Nonetheless, my boy, he's claimed you as a partner. The investigation will clear you of wrongdoing, I'm certain, but we thought you should be advised."

Investigation. The whole town was about to learn some ugly things about a builder they'd come to trust. He might as well pack his bags and find another place to hide.

"This is partly my fault," he said. "I thought he might be up to something illegal."

"Yet, you continued to let him live in your lovely home. Pray tell, Jace Carter, why would you do that?"

"I couldn't prove anything and I—" He clenched and unclenched his fist. "Selfish reasons."

The two old men exchanged glances. Popbottle Jones spoke. "You may be surprised to discover what two nosy old men with too much time on their hands already know. But we'd like to hear the details from you."

Jace opened his mouth to tell them, when down the street, a siren revved up in a spine-tingling wail. All three men looked in that direction. The siren grew louder and a gleaming red fire engine rounded the corner and headed north.

"Bad day for a fire."

"Is there ever a good day for one?"

Jace's cell phone rang. Glad for the distraction, he answered. Donny's voice came over the line.

"Jace, old buddy, I gotta hit the road. Just wanted to say bye. Sorry about your lady. Like you said, she was too good for you."

Jace gripped the receiver the way he wanted to grip Donny's neck. "You creep, where are you? You're not running out now. These people trusted you."

Donny laughed. "No way, amigo. They trusted *you*. Ironic, isn't it?"

"Don't do this, Donny. Give back the money. I'll help you any way I can, but don't do this to Redemption."

"Too late, bro, I already have. Oh, and hey." His tone was chipper. "You better get home. I think your house is on fire."

Kitty closed the office early and went to her cottage. The headache pounded with such intensity, she took two aspirin and lay down. She'd never had a migraine in her life, but this one qualified. Images of the day rushed behind her eyelids, making the headache pound harder. She moaned and pulled the pillow over her face.

She'd made a mess of everything. When she'd prayed about Jace, she'd had such a peace. She'd truly believed he was right for her. She struggled to accept the truth both Donny and Jace had revealed. Jace had been in prison.

Why hadn't he told her? Why hadn't he told anyone?

Was he, as Donny insisted, still living a life of crime?

She flopped over on her side. Her stomach heaved.

Jace ran a reputable business. He'd invested his own money and time to do something wonderful for this town. He was not a criminal. He was gentle and kind and he loved her. She was certain of that. No man could pretend the tenderness with which he'd kissed her.

Trina, too, had claimed Jace only wanted her for the motel. Could both Donny and Trina be wrong?

But Donny's claims seemed far-fetched, an almost desperate attempt to turn her against Jace. She no more believed Donny was a U.S. Marshal than she believed Jace was a criminal.

"Jesus," she whispered, too weary and confused to say more. He would know what she needed. The Lord was her strength and her redeemer, her ever-present help in a time of trouble. And boy, did she have trouble.

A knock sounded at her door.

"Go away." She knew no one could hear her from the bedroom. The knock came again, more insistent. A muffled voice called, "Miss Kitty, are you in there?"

Only one person in Redemption called her Miss Kitty. GI Jack. Dizzy, she stumbled to the door, holding her forehead.

Popbottle Jones and GI Jack stood at her door, panting like puppy dogs. Concern wrinkled their faces. "My dear lady, are you ill?"

"Headache," she managed. The dizziness subsided. She blinked to clear her vision. "I'm sorry. Would you like to come in? I must look terrible."

"You're lovely as always." Popbottle Jones stepped over the threshold.

GI Jack followed, taking off his cap which he twisted in his hands. "Miss Kitty, we got some bad news."

She wasn't sure she could take anymore. She swayed.

"GI, take her arm. She needs to sit down."

The two gentlemen led her to the couch, then stood uncertainly in front of her. "May I get something for you? Some water? Tea perhaps?"

She started to shake her head but thought better of it. "I'm feeling better now. A headache. What's this bad news? Is this about Jace?"

"Yes, I fear it is."

"I already know. He told me. Or rather Donny Babcock broke the news."

The Dumpster divers exchanged glances. "He told you what?"

Kitty rested her forehead on the heel of her hand. Her brain was mush. "He was in prison. I know. And he's going back."

"Going back? I think not. Jace Carter has done no wrong."

She looked up, uncomprehending. "He hasn't?"

"My dear lady, I am unaware of what conspired between you and Donny Babcock, but you seem to be under a false impression. Let me allay your concerns. Donny Babcock is the criminal. His investment schemes are just that, schemes. Jace Carter is a fine, upstanding citizen caught in a sinister ploy while trying to do the right thing."

"He is?"

"Indeed he is. Donny Babcock came to Redemption under false pretenses and Jace took him in, hoping to help the scoundrel turn a new leaf."

"Yep. That's right, Miss Kitty." GI's head bobbed. "Right as rain. Donny suckered everyone. Even the man who tried to help him get straight."

"Jace was in prison. He told me so himself."

"He was indeed. He paid his debt to society years ago and moved to Redemption a redeemed soul."

Kitty's hand went to her lips. "Oh, my goodness. Oh, thank the Lord. Why didn't he tell me?"

"I think you know the answer. Shame. Regret. Goc made him a new man and Redemption gave him a new beginning. Why look back?"

Yet he had. The light came on inside Kitty's muzzy head. Jace said he'd loved her for a long time. Now she understood. He'd loved her and been afraid of exactly this. Rejection.

"I have to see him." She started to rise. A wave of dizziness pushed her down again.

"You better rest yourself, Miss Kitty. You're looking poorly."

"No, you wanted to tell me something."

The pair exchanged glances. She knew that look.

"Our news can wait."

"No, it can't. I'm not some puny woman who can't tolerate a little headache. Tell me."

GI Jack grinned. "That's what I like about you. Spunk. You're a good fit for Jace Carter." He nodded. "Yep. Good fit."

"Before my loquacious friend bloviates you into unconsciousness, I will relay the bad news. There has been a fire at Jace's home."

A man could only take so much before he cracked Jace thought he might be at that point.

Smoke and flames billowed from the Queen Anne. His beautiful Queen Anne.

Milo was in there.

Adrenaline jacked to Mach speed, he leaped from the truck, running. Firefighters in yellow gear were already blasting water on the fish scale shingles. Flames crept up the outside.

"My dog's inside," he yelled to the first firefighter he saw. He bolted toward the front door only to have powerful arms pull him back.

"We'll get him. Stay put. Don't want to rescue you, too."

The tall, muscular fireman, Zak Ashford, yelled to the others and then breached the front door. Smoke billowed out.

Jace's beat erratically at the thought of little Milo inside that house. He found himself chanting, "God, let him be all right. Let him be all right."

His prayer was answered when Zak rushed onto the porch, smoke trailing him, Milo against his chest.

Zak stripped away his air mask and grinned. Soot framed his mouth. "Here you go. He came right to me. Shaking like a leaf."

Shaking a little himself, Jace accepted the frightened puppy. Though he smelled of smoke and his eyes and nose ran, Milo appeared to be okay. He scooted up Jace's shirt and buried his whimpering muzzle in his master's neck.

"How bad it is in there?"

Another engine pulled in just then and two more men leaped out, pulling hose around the house.

"Cody and Matt are assessing. Looks like the flames are confined to one room. That's all I saw. Not too bad yet. Someone must have spotted the smoke and called it in before the fire got out of hand."

"It looks out of hand to me."

An ax slammed against the fish scale roof. His heart sunk like Kitty's skipping rocks had sunk in the pond. He'd spent a boatload of money and many man hours on that roof but that wasn't the worst of it. This was home. The home he'd wanted with all his heart. The home he'd dreamed of sharing with Kitty.

The firefighter thumped him on the shoulder. Green eyes stood out in a face stained with soot. "Hang tough, buddy. We'll knock it down pretty fast if the wind doesn't get up."

"I'll hold you to that."

Zak shot him a cocky grin. "Ten minutes flat or I'll buy you dinner."

"You're on."

With a swagger of confidence born of being good at his job, Zak jogged off, gear rattling, to join the other firefighters.

Ten minutes later he was back. "You owe me dinner. T-bone steak."

Even with his heart broken, his life in disarray, and one room of his house a soggy mess of soot and ash, Jace appreciated the firemen's work. "Worth every penny. Thanks, Zak."

The firefighter saluted. "Doing my duty. Glad we made it in time." He ruffled Milo's ears. "It would be a shame to lose a place like this."

But lose it Jace would. The house and land was the only thing of value he owned. Donny had pawned Kitty's motel and he had no doubt the loan payoff

...ld be exorbitant. Jace was not going to let Kitty ...se the motel. He couldn't give her much, but he ...ould give her that.

"Know anyone who wants to buy one slightly damaged, mostly restored Queen Anne?"

Two hours later the fire trucks were gone, the *Register* reporter had taken photos and left, and Jace worked alone in the room Donny had slept in. The ceiling still dripped water from the gaping hole chopped by a firefighter's ax. One wall was completely gutted and the sun shone in through the opening. He'd have to go into town later for some plastic to cover the holes.

According to the preliminary report, the fire had started here, in the center of the room. Only one thing made sense. Arson.

He knew the guilty party was Donny. What he didn't know was why. Why did Donny hate him enough to drag his name through the mud, hurt the people he cared about, and torch his house?

It didn't make sense.

Hands on his hips, he shook his head. Life didn't make sense.

Using the shovel and wheelbarrow he'd brought from the shop, he started scooping. Nothing much in the room worth saving anyway. A pile of burned papers, a melted vinyl air mattress, and the little dab of furniture Donny had bought was collapsed in a heap.

Milo sniffed around the charred wet mess t stayed close to Jace's feet. The scare had shaken hi and now he didn't want Jace out of his sight.

Heart heavy and sad, he figured he should get word to Ned. The teen had gone into town this morning to meet friends and hang out at the festival. No telling when he'd come home.

Jace huffed. Home.

By tomorrow, the news about Donny's scam would break and with it the story of Jace Carter. He knew how newspeople worked. They'd want to know everything about Donny Babcock. Why he'd come to Redemption. How he'd known Jace Carter. If Donny hadn't already spread the word, the news media would put two and two together.

Rebuilding this room shouldn't take too long. He was thankful the flames hadn't touched the living room. That room alone had taken months and was a strong selling point. With the main interior complete, he could put the Queen Anne up for sale.

He hurt to even think about it.

A car door slammed outside. Ned must have found a ride. Milo tiptoed to the hole in the wall, peeked out and whined.

Jace leaned the shovel against the wheelbarrow. Ned would be upset. He'd better go.

Stripping dirty gloves from his hands, he stepped through the hole in the wall with Milo tight at his heel.

Kitty came striding toward him.

His heart stopped, started again. He tried to breath. What was she doing here?

"Jace Carter, I have something to say to you."

He was sure she did. And he had it coming. He'd brought her nothing but trouble. He braced himself, feet apart, for the blast he deserved. She kept coming, never slowing her pace. She was three feet away. Then two. Then one. And still she came.

In the next instant, she bumped into his chest and put her arms around him. "I love you."

He thought he'd crumple then and there. Nothing had prepared him for this, for her steadfast, unfailing, unwavering love. His arms went around her, gathered her close. He breathed her in, knowing this was crazy and in a minute, he'd wake up. The smoke inhalation must have gotten to him.

"You can't." Her hair smelled like flowers and was just as soft.

"Too bad because I do. If you think a little thing like a prison record, *fifteen years ago* when you were a kid, is going to change that, then you don't know me very well."

She pulled back a little and he saw the grit in her blue eyes. He'd thought her fragile and delicate but she was stronger than he'd ever be.

"I'm an ex-con. A worthless excuse of a human. You're a hero's widow. You deserve better. All I've done is cause you grief."

"What you've done is wake me from a very long sleep. I was in limbo, Jace, until you came along

and stirred my heart again. Dave would never ha
wanted me to live in the past. And that's what you'r
doing, too."

"I am?"

"Yes, so stop it. I care about now, about the good
and honorable man you are now." Blue eyes going
tender, she placed a soft hand on his cheek. That
simple touch sent a shiver through his body. "You
love me, don't you?"

"More than anything."

"Okay then. There you are. I'm yours. You're mine.
I have a headache. So shut up and kiss me."

Jace laughed. How could he not? She was the cutest
woman on the planet. He kissed her.

The ice around his heart melted into a puddle, no
match for the warmth of Kitty's love.

When the kiss ended, he held her for a little while,
soaking up the love she offered. He couldn't believe
this was happening.

Milo milled around their feet but neither paid him
any mind. They basked in the glow of love finally
realized. Jace couldn't get enough of holding her. He
wanted to forget about the burned house and Donny's
scam, but he couldn't. Both issues needed resolution
before he and Kitty could move forward.

Reluctantly, he pulled away and took her hand and
led her to the front porch where they sat on the bottom
step.

"I'm glad the porch didn't burn," she said.

"Me, too." The curving wraparound was the

.erior's centerpiece, restored to white perfection.
. think Donny set the fire."

"I'm so sorry, Jace, but I suspected as much. He came to see me today. He acted…strange." She turned his hand over and kissed the scars. She knew. He could tell she knew. A little quiver ran through him that she loved him anyway.

"What did he say?"

She told him everything, from Donny's bizarre declaration of love to the accusations against Jace. When she told him about the U.S. Marshal's badge, he laughed—a rueful, angry bark of sound.

"He's no more a U.S. Marshal than I am. We were in prison together. I doubt he told you that."

"No, he didn't."

"He stole from you, Kitty."

"GI Jack and Popbottle Jones told me. I'm so mad I could cry, but God will not let Donny Babcock get away with this."

"I hope you're right." Please Lord, let her be right.

She squeezed his hand, then opened it and traced the scars with her fingertip. "Donny said— These aren't the only ones, are they?"

He swallowed. "No."

"Tell me about it, Jace. What happened? How did you end up in such a terrible situation?"

Night was crowding in, that dusky, silvery time when lightning bugs began to flicker and frogs began to croak. Jace longed for the blackness to be complete. Talking in the dark was easier.

But he'd lived in darkness long enough. It was time for the truth to come into the light. It was time to be free.

And so, there on the porch with her soft hand holding his, her gentle voice asking the right questions, and her love holding his world in focus, he told her every ugly detail of the man he'd been, about the fights that nearly killed him, about a mentor who'd led him toward the Lord and of the redemptive love of God that had brought him out and made him new.

When he'd finished, Kitty cupped his face and kissed him with a sweet compassion that made him love her all the more.

"Show me," she whispered against his cheek.

He knew she meant the scars. He pulled back, scared. "No. I—they're—"

How did he explain how revolted she would be?

"Show me, Jace," she demanded again, a hand on his chest. "Show me so you can stop worrying about my reaction."

He shook his head. "I don't know if I can."

Kitty ran a soft hand over his shoulders. "Here?"

He nodded.

She scooted around behind him. Her hand moved over his back. "Here?"

"Across the shoulder, down the side, and across my back. Torres was in the pen for slicing people up. He liked doing it."

Her hand stilled. He felt her there as she leaned her forehead against him, her breath warm through his

rt. "Oh, Jace. I love you so much. I'm sorry for all
ou've been through."

"My own fault."

He felt the softness of her lips against his back.
"Paid in full. Jesus has scars, too, you know, and He
got them so you and I could let ours go. Let them go,
Jace."

He knew she was right. Until he could let her see
the shameful scars, he'd never believe she would love
him regardless.

Trembling inside, he pulled his shirt loose from
the back waistband of his jeans. Cool evening air
rushed against his skin, a drastic change from the
earlier heat of the fire. Funny how the fire seemed
so unimportant at the moment.

He knew when he'd lifted the shirt far enough,
though he could not see Kitty's face—and didn't want
to. What if she was horrified?

Soft fingers touched him. Jace shuddered.

"You're beautiful," she whispered. "Scars and all.
Maybe I love you more because of them, because of
what you've overcome to be the man you are."

Her love flowed into him, a healing balm to wipe
away the shame and regret of fifteen years. When
she gently tugged his shirt down, he remained with
hands on his knees, staring toward the pond where
he'd first known he was in over his head.

He wasn't a man to shed tears, wouldn't now,
though fullness clogged his throat and burned behind
his eyelids.

"Now you know why I had to help Donny." I made a sound of self-mockery. "Or tried to. No matte what he's done, I'd be dead if not for him. God gave me a second chance, and I thought Donny should have one, too. I tried, but I failed."

"Donny made that choice, Jace. You did what the Lord would have you do." Fabric rustled as she moved around to sit on the step in front of him. Her heart-shaped face tilted upward, full of tenderness. "You may not have helped Donny, but look at what you did for Ned. He's a different boy. *You* made that difference."

"See why I love you? You always say the right thing." He pulled her to him and kissed her nose.

When the sound of a car engine rumbled up the drive, Kitty and Jace broke apart. Kitty stood, peering into the semi-darkness.

"Who is that?"

Jace stood, too. He didn't recognize the vehicle or the driver, but a familiar shape sat in the passenger seat. "Not sure. Maybe someone bringing Ned home."

The car stopped and the engine died. The car was still rocking when Ned leaped out. Even in the twilight, his grin gleamed bright.

"Look what I found."

Jace turned curious eyes to the man exiting the driver's side. He looked vaguely familiar but Jace couldn't place him. Beside him, Kitty gasped.

"Oh, my goodness. Jace. It's Jerry Benedict."

Ned laughed and ran around the car to grab the river in a bear hug. "This is my brother. The man you tried to save from drowning in Redemption River."

Jace sat down on the porch with a stunned thud.

This had to be the strangest day of his life.

Epilogue

Three days later, Redemption was still abuzz with news. The *Register* couldn't decide whether to headline the return of Jerry Benedict from the dead or the embarrassing scam Donny Babcock had perpetrated.

In the end they'd run both as good news because the feds had captured Donny Babcock at the airport in Tulsa with most of the money in his possession. It would be a while before the victims got their money back, but they would get it.

The news was cause for celebration, but no one celebrated more than Jace. Kitty's motel loan had never been completed by the lender. And the man he couldn't save from drowning was back from the dead.

Jerry apparently had been swept far enough downstream that when he'd been found, no one suspected he was the victim from Redemption, and Jerry had been too ill to say. He'd developed some kind of brain

...ection from being in the water too long. Jace didn't ...egin to understand that, but a doctor had verified the illness. When he'd finally regained his health and come to himself, he'd found his way back to the place he belonged and the brother who mourned.

Ned was delirious with joy and Jace was happy for the teen. He needed family. Every man needed family.

Jace gazed around at the crowd of people roaming in and out of his house. They'd arrived with Kitty and Ned early this morning, bringing with them tools and materials, food and laughter. Without a word, other than asking for instructions from the builder, they'd gone to work, tearing out the old wall, ripping off burnt shingles, cleaning up the mess.

Kitty hooked a hand over his arm and snuggled against his side. "What do you think of all this?"

He was flabbergasted. Blessed. Shaken.

"Don't they know?"

"Every last one of them."

He shook his head. "And they don't care?"

"Yes, they do care. That's the point. They care about you."

Emotion clogged his throat. He didn't understand but he wasn't complaining.

"Why would they do this?"

"Same reason. Redemption is family, Jace. Your family."

"I actually planned to sell this house," he told her. "To repay that loan on your motel."

Kitty looked aghast. She whapped his arm. "___
way. I plan to sell that motel and live in this house___

"You do?"

She blushed. "Well, if you want me to."

Jace thought he'd probably died and gone to heaven. "Is this a proposal?"

"Maudie Underwood would swoon if she heard such a thing. A man asks a woman." She turned twinkling blue eyes on his. "So are you going to ask me?"

He took her hand, amused, but serious, too. "Kitty, I love you. I've loved you so long, I don't know where I end and you begin. Will you marry me and live in this big money pit with me? I promise to love you and take care of you and our babies as long as I live."

"Babies." She sighed. "Oh, yes."

Then she threw her arms around his neck and kissed him with enough fire and love to burn another house down.

Jace's chest expanded with pride and hope. He, a man of shame and regrets, looked out at the group of friends and neighbors who'd come because of him, because they cared, because they accepted him, sin and all.

And with God's help and the love of a hero's wife, he was finally able to accept himself.

"Hey!" a voice yelled. "You two gonna stand out there kissing all day?"

Jace laughed. Kitty blushed.

"Maybe."

Amidst the laughter and teasing, with joy in his heart, Jace took Kitty's hand and led the way back into the construction zone...back to the place where he finally, comfortably, completely belonged.

The old Queen Anne was getting her third chance at life.

And so was he.

* * * * *

Look for more books in the
REDEMPTION RIVER *series*
later this year, only from RITA award-winning
author Linda Goodnight.

Dear Reader,

The Bible has a number of references for the potter and clay, but for *A Place to Belong* I chose the verse in Jeremiah 18. In a way, this was Jace Carter's life verse. His bad choices as a youth had crushed him. God in his love and mercy had slowly rebuilt Jace into a man of worth and value. And yet, out of guilt and remorse, Jace struggled to accept this precious gift of God.

Are you like that sometimes? I know I am. It's hard to imagine that God loves me enough to overlook my mistakes and want the best for me. And yet He does.

Thank you for joining me in the small town of Redemption, Oklahoma. I hope you've enjoyed your visit and will come back again at Christmas for the next installment.

I am always happy to hear from readers. You may contact me at www.lindagoodnight.com or by mail through Steeple Hill, 233 Broadway, Suite 1001, New York, NY 10279.

Until the next time, God bless and happy reading.

Linda Goodnight

QUESTIONS FOR DISCUSSION

1. Who were the main characters in *A Place to Belong?* Did you like them? Who was your favorite? Why?

2. Choose one of the secondary characters and discuss his/her role in the story. What did he/she add to the plot? Was his/her role essential or could anyone have filled it?

3. Even though her husband has been dead for seven years, Kitty Wainwright can't move on. Why do you think she reacts this way? Is it grief, fear, or some other emotion that keeps her stuck in the past?

4. Have you ever known anyone like Kitty? Did that person ever get over his/her grief?

5. Have you ever lost a loved one? How did you cope?

6. Jace Carter hides his past but refuses to have his scars removed. Why? What do you think the scars symbolize?

7. Jace and Kitty are both stuck in the past. Com-

pare and contrast the two. Then discuss how each one helps the other move forward.

8. When Donny Babcock arrives in Redemption, why does Jace feel compelled to help him? What would you have done in that situation? Does Scripture obligate a Christian in this way? Can you find a Bible verse to support your answer?

9. Do you think Donny Babcock was sincere when he claimed to be a Christian? Or was he using this as a con? Site specific instances in the story to support your answer.

10. Jace applies the parable of reaping and sowing to his past mistakes. Do you believe a person will reap what he sows? What does this mean? Can a sinner ever repay the wrong he's done? How can someone in Jace's situation ever feel completely "clean" again?

11. Redemption is known as a place where hurting people come to heal. Jace lived in the small town for fourteen years and yet, he was still wounded. Why do you suppose that's true?

12. Jace's greatest fear was the revelation of his past mistakes. Was this a legitimate concern? Can a person ever completely shed a sinful past?

How would you react if an ex-con moved in next door to you?

13. Why do you suppose Kitty's in-laws wanted her to remain single? Why did they feel threatened by Jace? Who did you empathize with, Kitty or the grieving parents? Was there right and wrong on both sides? Discuss.

14. Was there any part of the story you would change if you could? If so, what was it and how would you change it?

15. The Scripture verse from Jeremiah 18 is true for this book on several levels. How does it relate to Jace? How does it relate to the career path he chose? Do you see a parallel with Ned Veech as well? What about the broken-heart box GI Jack creates for Kitty?

LARGER-PRINT BOOKS!

GET 2 FREE
LARGER-PRINT NOVELS
PLUS 2 FREE
MYSTERY GIFTS

Love Inspired®

Larger-print novels are now available...

LILPI1

SUSPENSE

RIVETING INSPIRATIONAL ROMANCE

Watch for our series of edge-
of-your-seat suspense novels.
These contemporary tales
of intrigue and romance
feature Christian characters
facing challenges to their faith...
and their lives!

AVAILABLE IN REGULAR
& LARGER-PRINT FORMATS

For exciting stories that reflect traditional values,
visit:
www.ReaderService.com